Monster

Monster

Ashleigh Synnott

PUNCHER & WATTMANN

First published in 2021

Published by Puncher and Wattmann
PO Box 279
Waratah NSW 2298

fiction@puncherandwattmann.com

NATIONAL
LIBRARY
OF AUSTRALIA

A catalogue entry for this book is available from the National Library of Australia.

ISBN   9781925780994

Cover design by Miranda Douglas

Printed by Lightning Source International

This project has been assisted by the Australian Government through the Australia Council, its arts funding and advisory body.

Australian Government

Australia Council
for the Arts

Contents

The Trial

Cassandra was a priestess of Apollo in Greek mythology. She saw true things no one believed. She had brown eyes and was considered insane. I think she would have really liked emojis.

My true feeling is she would have liked the happy ghost, if she had to choose one. She would have used the green pistol to punctuate every narrative describing the same-old, same-old story of her life – how she saw true things no one believed. But I am not so interested in this aspect of the narrative. I mean it would be pretty bad to be so sure of certain things only to be labelled mad upon their utterance and imprisoned in a pyramid on the citadel on the orders of your father, King Priam. I mean certainly that would have been frustrating but also it's not that interesting because everybody who says stuff they feel strongly about, even if that stuff is not true, wants to be taken seriously.

No, what interests me about Cassandra is the way she resolved – nay, determined – the hierarchy of suffering in her life. How she experienced going from predicted crisis to predicted crisis interspersed only with actual crisis, as predicted, and a little brutal rape.

Like, how did she alter her mode of expression? Did she increase the urgency in her tone as she went along in her life or did she grow tired and resigned to the mountains of horror, spurting the information out in sharp bursts like the cunjevoi do water, but basically otherwise just quietly accepting her fate as a delicious sea-squirt covered in green-brown algae with a tough brown tunic on intertidal rocky shores for the rest of the time?

Also was she surprised, each time, by the drama? Did the hell of it remain fresh, even to her who had seen so much hell? Did she relay what would prove to be historically accurate information regarding the Trojan War with the horse and the sword and the shrug emoji blonde or did she put her hands over her ears at any stage and scream no? Or did she do the screaming inside her head so no one could disbelieve her, re: the screams? Or did she text Ajax so late at night just with: Pls bring the statue, baby xxxx.

The ancient Greeks had to go the long way about things. Blue gummy bears, unfortunately, had not yet been invented but I hope Cassandra also saw happy future things, like blue gummy bears. And a GIF of a kid with a bowl haircut waving a spatula which says so very much in these troubled times.

Also I am totally interested in her personal experience of so much catastrophe? Was there some point at which she thought well, these things might occur but they don't personally concern me and if I go ahead and get involved again, vis-à-vis communicating what I see, I myself might have to endure a degree of personal suffering at least commensurate with the suffering of the others I foresee so I am going to put up some personal boundaries here and although I feel a social responsibility to warn my fellow citizens of the dangers they do face, I am going to take heed of the fact that I basically get *persecuted* every time I try to *help* so in this instance I might just keep my mouth *shut*? I mean, maybe dabble in a fig and pass the arvo that way?

No, but wait.

What I really want to know is how she reacted internally to the news, every time it came to her first. Like when she foresaw who Paris really was and that his penis was not much bigger than his apple, was she self-conscious regarding this vision or was she curious in an historically detached and socially acceptable manner? Certainly she loved that he was suckled by a she-bear! But such details aside, when she proclaimed him her abandoned brother, was she kind of excited to be the bearer of such big news in the context of initiating familial reparations or did she carry this information as a terrible weight, linked as it was to the abduction of Helen by her unstable but kind of hot sibling, and the Trojan War?

The mythological fact that tells me everything I need to know is that while the people rejoiced, Cassandra snatched away Helen's golden veil and tore at her hair and this is the point at which matters of the imagination become physical confrontations. And enter the realm of reality that way.

I mean I'm not exactly saying violence is ever an appropriate art but when Cassandra tore at Helen's veil I thought, huh. I thought, at least this woman is taking reality into her own hands instead of waiting, just waiting, for someone to believe.

I guess if she were my friend I would text her the crown as a kind of bitter joke? Or maybe a couple of rainbows like hint hint or just those three little green leaves fluttering down as a way to say oh … well … life … ends up here.

Violence is not a way to solve things I know but once when I was on the bus, when I'd just got on the bus and was up the back and looking for a seat and there were all these girls in private school uniforms, sitting one girl to a seat in their blue blazers and blue skirts, each with one leg bent up on the seat so the full pale calf and knee of each girl was visible, except where the legs were rudely cut off by the white socks with the little emblem on them, which was in the shape of a crown and navy blue to match the blazers and the heavy, longish skirts, I stood in the aisle, facing this one girl, who looked up at me, and I looked down at her, and she did not move her lovely leg, which she had bent to take up as much space as possible on the bus seat like the rest of the girls and I said, move please I need to sit down. Because those were the rules of the bus.

And this golden-haired child just looked up at me. She was maybe fifteen and I was fifteen and she looked up at me with her pretty, open face, just smiling, and she looked around at the rest of the girls, who also smiled, and she did not move her leg.

And I waited several long seconds for this girl to move her leg but all she did was smile and she did not move her leg so even though I am not a violent person in the traditional sense I put my own knee on the seat and I put one hand on the back of the seat and with the other hand I reached, grabbed a fistful of her hair and snapped her head smartly back. The shape of her pretty face slightly changed.

'Listen, honey,' I said.

She listened to what I said. And I let go.

She shifted her knee. And I sat down.

Yeah, yeah I know it was only a dream but when I woke up I was so bloody pleased I had finally done something with all my physical strength to change the course of my life and that bus trip and ancient history and everything. Dream or no dream it was some place to start.

Things of Love

Libby was eight and she had never had a friend but so far as she could see she wasn't missing anything. She had her mother.

'Can you believe all that used to be inside her?' Nancy said.

The host in tight jeans was pulling a kart of fat across the stage.

'That is actual dedication,' Nancy said. 'That's an average ten-year-old child in fat, Elizabeth. Are you looking at this?'

Libby worked her fingers in Nancy's long hair.

'You could do it,' Libby said.

'I don't know,' Nancy said.

'You could do it,' Libby said. 'I firmly believe you can do anything.'

While Jeff and Libby ate in front of the television, Nancy studied the book which informed her new life.

'I do not understand why potatoes are bad,' she said. 'Peanut butter has eight grams of fat per tablespoon. One small potato has only zero point two. This is what I do not understand.'

'It's the carbs,' Jeff said, licking his knife.

'But carbohydrates are not fat,' Nancy said, checking her book. 'It's a different column.'

'Carbs turn to fat,' Jeff said. 'Check this guy out.'

A man with clown hair on the television was waving a gong, threatening to end the performance on stage. The performance was a trio of little girls in ballet skirts singing a popular song. The thing was each of them was holding a bearded dragon.

'Look at this guy. He's a prick. Here he goes.'

The man sounded the gong. The audience groaned. One of the dragons puffed out his beard.

Nancy cut out bread, potatoes, sugar, pumpkin, yoghurt, butter, fruit and dinner. She sipped lemon and warm water. She practiced sit-ups.

'Nothing tastes as good as thin feels,' Nancy said. 'And it's true.'

She was trying on jeans. Libby clapped her hands. She sat at the end of the change room in an upholstered chair, where she found that if she restricted her vision by closing one eye she couldn't tell her real mother from the one in the glass.

'Oh Nancy,' she said. 'They look good, they look good.'

'You say that every time,' Nancy said, turning to the side. But she was smiling.

To celebrate Nancy's incredible weight loss, Jeff took them on the train to the quay. They saw a silver man. They saw a seal on the steps surrounded by police. Outside the museum there was a man doing cartoons. Jeff pushed through the crowd, pulling Nancy along.

'Do us,' he said. 'How much for us?'

The man looked up. Libby saw he was working on a portrait of the Queen but he had only completed half of the head.

'You'll have to sit close,' the man said. 'So I can get you all in.'

Jeff sat on the stool, Nancy on his lap. Libby stood in the centre. She watched the man work. Behind him the sun was setting over the water, the boats.

'Don't move,' the man said. 'Keep smiling. That's it.'

Libby's face hurt from smiling. The boats came and went. The seal hissed.

Close to Christmas, Nancy plateaued.

'Useless, useless,' she said.

'It's all right,' Jeff said. 'You can do this, baby. If you get down to an eight, we'll get married again.'

'I don't even know what that would mean,' Nancy said.

'I'll hire a room at the club and we'll invite everyone. We'll have streamers and balloons. Good quality champagne. You'll wear the kind of dress you should have worn before and we'll get someone to marry us all over again. Think of it.'

'Wow,' Nancy said.

'I love you,' Jeff said. 'I want everyone to know and share in that love.'

'A size eight,' Nancy said. 'What would that even mean?'

'It's only discipline,' Jeff said. 'Like anything.'

Libby went outside to get the washing in. The light went out so late in those long summer days when the scream of the black princes, the greengrocers, filled the streets. Here was a greengrocer, body parts missing again. The bull ants had worked him, they'd removed all his legs, but his shining black eyes still caught everything. Libby picked up the grocer and held him in the palm of her hand. Then she opened her mouth. He buzzed on her tongue. He squirmed, then was still. Libby turned her eyes to the festering sky and finished him in two neat, clean bites.

The wedding took place the following spring. Libby was nine and wore a black dress.

'I never thought I'd be the kind of guy to marry twice,' Jeff said.

Everyone cheered.

'Here's to my new wife. Will you just look at her?'

Nancy smiled and smiled. She sipped her champagne. Libby closed her eyes. She thought she could hear, somewhere, the sound of the moon. It was outside the window – singing, buzzing. It was the sound, she decided, of certain things of love as they came to fresh life in the dead centre of herself. She opened her eyes wide to take in the whole scene. It was clear to her that something big was missing but she couldn't make it out just yet. Everybody was there.

Story of a Gumtree

There's a gumtree, an extremely large one, right outside my window. It is so large it gets stuck to all the other trees. Possums live there, or so Helen said. She'd walked around the place acting the part, clicking her tongue and nodding at the front room, the bathroom and the kitchen with the marble bench top that looked like real marble but which I had already melted a hole in with the coffee pot. Now she was standing at the back window looking out into the yard. Dusk was just getting started.

'Oh,' she said. 'Will you look at that tree.'

I was standing in the kitchen holding onto the door of the refrigerator. The outline of her body against the pink and grey light coming through the window had an effect on me and I had an idea of what I'd like to do with her now. I was particularly taken with the bare back of her pale knees and the dirt around her heels where the straps had rubbed in.

'Apparently there's possums,' I said, letting go the fridge door.

I stood close behind her with both hands on her hips and my face in her neck. It was hot. She wore a cheap vanilla oil which filled my head fast but was sour on my tongue. There was dirt on the windowsill from somebody else's plants and a spider's web, torn down. Helen stepped away and opened the back door. She stood at the top of the steps looking at the tree, one hand on the railing.

'Oh yes,' she said. 'Yes. There would be possums for sure.'

I went back into the kitchen and took some olives from the fridge. They fell flat and cold into the bowl she had brought me for the house. I set the bowl on the table. I took the wine out of the fridge and the rum from the freezer and I filled a bowl with ice and set all this out. I filled her glass with wine and used my fingers to fill my glass with ice because I thought I'd wait, take my time, but as soon as she sat down I poured the rum and got started in:

'Listen,' I said. 'I think the whole thing's really clear. I think there's a certain amount we can talk about, but in the end I think it's clear. What I can manage.'

'I understand,' she said.

She took a sip of her wine but it caught her in the throat and she coughed until water streamed from her eyes. I offered to get her something but she waved her hand and I sat back down. She took another sip, more carefully this time, then she laughed and finished her wine all in one go and I relaxed because I could see now it would soon be over, this whole charade. I poured more out for both of us and put my hand on her knee.

'Gee you've got a hide,' she said.

Then she shook her head and pushed her glasses up her nose, and she laughed and she laughed and she laughed.

Perhaps she didn't laugh that much, perhaps it was the rum. I took a drink and it settled me. The thing was that day, I guess, she'd done this new thing with her hair. It was short and it showed the grey underneath and this disturbed me. When I leaned forward and turned my head to the side at a particular angle, I could see the top of her thighs beneath her black skirt. They had a crinkle to them and these small purple veins. I didn't mind them. The thing was the hair.

'Well it's a real Australian house,' she said. 'It's a real Australian house with that tree.'

'You've got to try these olives,' I said. 'Go on.'

Helen took an olive. That's what I really liked about her. My wife, towards the end, she wouldn't eat anything at all. I leaned over and kissed her. She pulled away, laughed again, took up another olive and put that one in. When all the olives were gone she worked one finger in the oil, knocking about all the pips.

At some point between this conversation and the steak, the dark came fully down. Helen had made a salad and while I was cooking she disappeared out the front door. I poured a fresh drink as soon as the door clicked shut and took it down fast because I thought she'd be back immediately. I turned the steak. When it was finished I set it on a wooden board to rest and cleared the coffee table of the olive bowl and other things. I crunched some ice and stared into the sink, waiting for her to return. I poured another drink. I took my time with this one. I put the radio on and sat down to take it in and that's when Helen came back with all these orange flowers which she rinsed and tore up and put in the salad. I took up the steak and cutlery and set it all on the table. Helen sat down beside me and reached for the knife but her hands were shaking too much and I took it from her.

'Oh my god,' I said. 'What's the problem?'

I started going at the steak, cutting it into fine, neat, clean strips. Helen took up the remote and turned on the television but she was looking to her right, out the window, at the gumtree. That did it. I stood up and went into the kitchen to freshen my drink. I took a drink to steady myself but I was full on Sailor Jerry's, I was drinking to sober up, I was so full on Sailor Jerry's only more of it could help.

'Do we have to?' I said, sitting back down on the lounge.

So Helen turned the television off and in the quiet that came next I suddenly had a strange feeling like it wasn't my house, like the house didn't have anything to do with me at all, like I didn't belong in the house and the house didn't want me there and also like I was about to beg for something when this wasn't the case. The food was on the table and Helen was beside me on the lounge and everything was happening like stacking boxes on a shelf, one next to the other, contained and very clear but the insides were a mystery. I was getting all ready to give it to her, what I had decided about the whole thing, but when I started in this way her lips took an ugly turn and she put her head in her hands and her shoulders moved as she cried. She spilled it all out about her husband and her kids gone away and I knew I should put my hand on her back, to console her, but she was wearing a summer dress and the straps on the dress badly irritated me.

The straps slipped about as she told me at length of her fears. It was so boring. She had a mole on the outline of her right shoulder blade which had three fine brown hairs growing out of it. I thought of taking each of these hairs and pulling them out, one by one. I thought of the baby – half her and half me – and this thought repulsed me physically in the way Christmas carols do when I can't stop listening.

'They'll be back,' I said. 'They love you and they'll be back.'

But we were drinking like lunatics and no one was coming back. Plus I knew by then love didn't have anything to do with it.

We forgot about the steak. Anyway it grew cold. Someone opened a packet of corn chips and that did the trick. We talked reasonably about our options to do with our relationship but then she fell asleep and I got to thinking what I could do with her now, out cold on my lounge in her strappy summer dress. Her breath was sloppy and wet because she was drunk and she cleared her throat occasionally as she slept. For the first time I saw we were really alone in the house. She was asleep on my lounge and she belonged to me, in the now, this included what was inside of her, and I had the strong, happy feeling I could destroy it all anytime I felt like it. I lay down to think this over in more detail. Then I fell asleep.

In the middle of the night I woke up with her head on my chest. I lay there for a few moments just breathing. My tongue was thick and there was a sour film over my teeth but my head was clear. I ran my hand over her hair, back and forth in this way, and went through in my mind exactly what I had done. I hadn't done anything in the end. I was so relieved.

'I've changed my mind,' I said, trying to make it sound right.

'Let's do it,' I said. 'It will be all ours this time. We'll call it something good and we'll be happy with it. What's the worst that can happen?'

It didn't take. I thought for a moment she was maybe asleep but then she sat up and felt around for her shoes. I got up and turned on the light.

'I've got to go,' she said. 'I've got to get home.'

She sat there a moment, using the tip of her finger to smooth one eyebrow and then the next. I saw the raw, pink flesh on the edge of her thumb where she'd worried the skin, pulled it all the way down, and I guess I had a feeling like love, something big opened up. But then she got up and walked out of the house and as she sat on the doorstep to do up her shoes I had a very clear, very unobstructed view of the mess of her hair.

I went back inside and turned the steak into the bin. I had the idea to do a significant clean but the steak was as far as I got. I opened a beer and took it into the lounge. Then I changed my mind and opened the back door. I finished the beer in the yard, walking back and forth on the strip of concrete under the stairs. I grew tired. I lay down on the grass and allowed my eyes to close, thinking something vague and desperate, wanting to suffocate it with sleep.

The night air had a specific effect on my face. It was quiet but the leaves moved and the whole thing gave me a feeling like there was room for me after all and I began to slip away. But then I had the small, hard feeling I was being watched. I opened my eyes. Above me the leaves of the gumtree were a rusty canopy, they flickered the moonlight back and forth through the leaves and in the centre of it all in the middle of a branch two still, black eyes peered down.

It didn't strike me right away exactly what she was but soon the shape of her became completely clear to me. I lay there like that, still as anything, looking up. And for a long time, it seemed to me, the possum looked frankly down.

Eva and Tobias

Eva loved Tobias, same as anyone, but he wasn't what she wanted so she left. She drove south. She stuck mostly to the left lane, closest to the cliff, and did not break the limit. Now and then, when she went around a bend, she saw herself adjusting the wheel and putting the car into the cliff. The little car would crumple. She'd swallow her shattered teeth. Her torso would fly out and her head would crack the screen but below all of that her legs would be pinned down, locked in their place by the wheel.

Eva drove as far south in the state as she could go and when she crossed the border Tobias occurred to her. She experienced a connection to him which sounded like two plates of metal colliding in the space between her lungs. Or perhaps it was hunger — she had driven through lunch. She'd stop, she decided, in the next country town.

At the Crown Motel Eva sat down on the bed. She considered the walls, a baby shade of pink. There was a desk in the room and a sink next to the bed, also pink but more in the way of musk — a penetrating, glandular pink. Eva had an ache in her skull that went right down her back. Tobias came in — he rolled so easily in. Tobias standing in his cot, wide-eyed after sleep, knocking the ball. The ball was plain wood, painted with silver stars, and it descended from the neck-tie of the cloth duck hanging on the wall. Tobias banged rhythmically in this critical way, alerting her to some serious situation. She snapped open her eyes and got up off the bed.

Eva drove along the highway. There was a hollow wind behind her eyes and a white window she had to close which rattled somewhere. The sky had grown dark by the time the restaurant appeared.

The restaurant was empty. It was one of those truck stops directly off the highway which is conveniently located but doesn't know what it's about. Everything was on the menu but the menu had been put together at different times with different fonts and as a result it didn't seem to say anything specific. The cloths on the tables were white and made of paper and the drink coasters were square with round edges and featured jokes. Eva picked up one coaster and found she knew the joke: What's big and grey and wears a mask? The elephantom of the opera. What did the grape say when the man trod on it? Nothing – it just let out a little wine. She chose a table. She sat down. Suddenly she couldn't recall if she had paid for the room at the Crown Motel and it came to her some man was after her life. She'd be found out any minute and get taken off, put in a boot, definitely raped, she'd get stabbed to death with a screwdriver and she'd feel it all as she died and she knew this was possible because she'd seen this happen once in a dramatic re-enactment on daytime television. The feeling was that this was inevitable, it was just a matter of scary time, but then she remembered making the payment and the feeling went away. She put her head in her hands, closed her eyes.

When Eva looked up she saw a family had arrived. They were seated at the table directly across from her, and they were fat. The whole family was fat. There was a man, a woman, a teenage girl and a boy. The boy was the fattest. It was spectacular, Eva thought, how fat the boy was.

A bell dinged.

Eva watched, mesmerised, as the waitress delivered the family their food. Then she waited to see what the family would do. They ate. As individual people they ate but as a group they ate the food like a glorious machine. The man finished a hamburger, straight off. The woman did the same. Then she buttered rolls for the soup. The girl moved with terrific stealth between the lamb cutlets and the Buffalo wings.

The boy wasn't eating anything, apparently. His face was expressionless but he was doing something with his left hand underneath the table. His right hand was where anyone could see but his left hand was making a stabbing action, under the table.

'He's doing it again,' the girl said, scraping back her chair.

She stood over the table with a grin on her face.

'He's doing it again, Frank. He's doing it again.'

The girl ducked with surprising speed under the table.

'I got it,' she said, stabbing a fork in the air. 'I got it, I proved it. I told you people so.'

'Stand up Walter,' the man said.

The boy held onto the chair and moved himself off. This was some big effort. It seemed to Eva that he left his self behind – that when he stepped towards the man his self remained on the chair, looking on.

The man took a hold of the boy's t-shirt and yanked it up, exposing a great, flabby abdomen which was marked just above the waistband with four bloody red punctures, evenly spaced. The man let the shirt go.

'Time out Walter,' he said.

The boy looked around, as if for the first time he understood where he was. The width of his face and the thickness of his chest and his handmade breasts seemed to look about, too.

'But where will I go?' he said. 'There's nowhere to go.'

The man tore at a cutlet. The woman dipped her head to the soup. The girl stabbed a wing in the direction of the door.

'There are seats at the entrance,' she said. 'You can do your thinking out there.'

The boy stood still a moment longer, waiting for something. Then he walked away.

On her way out of the restaurant Eva paused at the door. The boy was sitting on his hands, swinging his legs back and forth. The boy considered her, his pale eyes ice blue in his fat, white face. Then he accepted her hand. They left the restaurant easily, like old friends.

As Eva drove, the boy slept. His head collapsed now and then, pushing forward and sideways onto the window. Eva put her hand to his forehead and pushed it back up. It stayed put a moment before it dropped back down. She gave up, drove on.

In the parking lot of the Crown Motel Eva woke the boy. He climbed the stairs heavily, as if drugged. In the hotel room she lay him down on the bed. She took off his shoes and pulled the blanket over him. Then she lay down herself and fell asleep at once. In her sleep she saw a silver pool of what appeared to be glitter expand in the liquid dark out of which the shape of a sitting duck grew then burst, expectantly. In the middle of the silver burst, a child cried out in the night.

Ducks

My father saved my life twice. Once with his enormous hand, and once with a dog with one brown eye and one blue.

In the first instance I was two years old. There was nothing to it. I was feeding the ducks at the pond and then there I was, actually inside the pond. The way my mother told it I just toppled right in. But I can see now I would have had to have walked down. Down the bank into the cold, dirty water. Steadily down.

I have an idea what was in my mind as I made my way down. Ducks. I had a plan when I was small to find a creature of my own. I was going to find a warm, fluffy creature to hold and keep and love. Even if I had to drag this creature soaking wet and flapping and screaming into my life, even if I had to ignore the biological requirements of this creature and put a rope around this creature's neck and tether it to a post when it was wicked or sad, I was going to find a creature to call my own and I was going to love it. Of this I was absolutely sure.

I saw these creatures everywhere. I saw them in the sparrows that hopped all around the neighbourhood where I grew up and I bet I saw them in the ducks that day at the pond. I bet I went after those ducks with my fingers outstretched and slipped into the silent night.

There weren't any ducks down there. It was liquid and light. An endless, quiet green. Then, of course, the colours changed. Green gave way to darkness – a dark yellow, then brown, then a rather black. I opened my mouth to let that darkness in. It was thick, it was light, it was heavy, like me. I was sinking, certainly, closer and closer, towards the mud.

Next thing my father pulls me up by the hair. With his huge hairy hand he pulls me up through the green liquid roof into the cold, flashing blue air of that bright winter day.

There were four different kinds of birds when I went back to the pond. I didn't plan it. But when I arrived I knew I'd always been headed there. What shocked me was how shallow the water was at the edge of the pond and the reeds that grew out of there, on the bank, and the range of birds. There was a tall white bird with a thin orange beak which walked high up on its legs and which was maybe a duck. There was a white bird which was a duck but I was thinking goose. There was a brown bird which was definitely a duck and when it lifted its wings there was a flash of emerald green. There was also an ibis, shameless, among the ducks.

Then it came to me that something was going on. On the surface of the pond, one white duck was on top of another white duck. The duck on the top was pulling at the hair on the head of the duck on the bottom and the duck on the bottom was just taking it. My first thought was they were mating – that the day was so uncharacteristically warm, they were acting as though spring was here. My second thought was how could you? How could you, you stupid ducks! It just seemed totally unfathomable that these ducks should be fucking, on my watch.

Well he rode her and rode her. And then a brown duck came along and got on top of the first guy, so now there were three ducks swimming around, two of them riding. They covered some distance in the pond arranged like this and no one looked twice. With their beaks in the air and their tail feathers going wiggle wiggle. Extraordinary!

The brown duck got off first and then the white duck shortly after. The bottom duck swam away and the white guy, well he reared up and started flapping and pumping his wings like mad.

I tried to focus on other things. The colour of the dead grass. The plaque at the bottom of a tree near the pond with somebody's beautiful daughter's name engraved on it. I tried to focus on the way the water rippled away from all the other ducks. I tried to imagine what their little legs looked like pumping under the water – but then, with no warning, one white duck was on top of another white duck and the same thing was happening in front of my eyes all over again.

I couldn't tell if they were the same ducks. They looked the same.

Sometimes the attempts were not successful. As in the procedure didn't last. But I watched and waited for the pull on the hair. Of course, it wasn't hair. Feathers? And anyway what was I doing, like some pervert, standing on the bank of the pond watching them?

When I got home I looked it up. I couldn't find any information on the white ducks specifically. All the information said there should be some sophisticated mating display but I didn't see any display, there was no pre-sex show, all I saw was the one duck on top of the other duck yanking at her hair and after he was finished he stood up in the water and pumped his wings in celebration.

I learned that some ducks have a spiral penis. I learned that other ducks don't have a penis, they just rub themselves together to make babies. I thought, there are congruencies here but what can I make of them? I thought, a little bit about ducks doesn't make a story.

Then I had myself an original idea. In the middle of the duck pond was an island. This island was dense with paperbark trees. I decided I would return in the middle of the night. The ducks would be asleep and the moon would be dead and I'd enter into that same water where I nearly died the first time and I would see what happened once I was under there.

With no cars on the road it didn't take long from my place. I parked out the front of the big houses. The street lights bared down. I left the key in the ignition and stepped out. I walked down the hill. I walked through the trees.

It was all quiet when I arrived at the pond. I slipped my jumper off. I took off my t-shirt, my bra. I took off my boots, my jeans. I took off my underwear. I didn't have any idea where the ducks slept but I hoped that I didn't disturb any sleeping ducks in the reeds as I made my way into the pond because the last thing I wanted was the sound of a duck waking from slumber or the sensation of a soft body, surprised, between my toes. For this reason, perhaps, I kept my socks on.

Fuck it was cold.

Under the water I opened my eyes. There was nothing. It was dark and it moved a little, it was quiet, perhaps I detected the sound of bubbles, trapped air, but apart from all this there was absolutely nothing. This surprised me.

When I surfaced I heard the sound of my own breath making its way across the icy water. I swam out to the island without any trouble. I climbed up the bank through more reeds. The bank was soft and gave like rotting flesh and I moved, moved further on, it was suddenly crucial to be inside the thickness of the trees and to see what I could see when I looked out.

Well, I just saw the pond. There were too many leaves and branches to see the sky. On the pond the light played from the streetlights. Everything was wet and I started to shiver. It started with my teeth and I had a recollection of being in a man's office. The man was drinking coffee from a mug and I was crying so hard my teeth slammed together, like this.

Time passed. I grew steadily colder, which was painful. At some point I got to the coldest I have ever been but then I stayed from then on exactly that cold and there came certain moments in that cold when I didn't feel quite so cold. Or at least I didn't think I did. And that's the same.

Something about the whole thing seemed a little disappointing. I guess I had expected something much more. Rats? I didn't expect to see any ducks. They were sleeping somewhere. I didn't hear any movement in the trees. They were all standing around like they were expecting something, too, but all in all they were much more accepting than me. They didn't fight.

I fought some but only a little. I sat up at first and then I lay down. I sat up again. I tried to get comfortable. Once or twice I thought, I wish I was dry. I bit my lower lip at the intense discomfort of the psoriasis on my elbow, which played up when it was wet. What was I doing, I thought. I hated being wet. I recollected. When I was a child I would eat the curtain. I'd cry at the window and while I was doing it I'd shove fistfuls of white curtain into my mouth.

I stopped recollecting. That's enough, I thought. That's enough. I decided, instead, that I would simply sit. I would sit and sit on the island like a mature adult. I would sit and wait and see what happened after that and whatever happened I would respond to it reasonably, without emotion.

Nothing happened. It was cold. I was wet. There was movement in the trees as the black began to lift, like the leaves were giving something in response to the rising sun and this made me feel guilty and so ungrateful of the dawn. I thought I should go out there to witness the sunrise, but then I worried I might be detected by some early morning jogger, so I stayed where I was, among the paperbark trees. I wondered if anyone tended this island and if I'd have to get a stick into them when they came. It suddenly occurred to me how long I had waited to get to where I was, sitting still, finally hidden. I tried to think of the first person who would notice I was gone.

Then the stupid ducks came out. They filed out like school children in the blue light before dawn. Like this was their thing. They entered the water. Most of them swam around, they weren't doing anything, they were probably peddling furiously under the water but they just carried on with these looks on their faces that said, I belong here, I belong here.

I admit, I reacted. I did not hesitate. I entered the pond.

The ducks went wild. I went wild after them. I was not calculated in my approach. I was not judicious. There was water and wings and noise and feathers and hurt. God, there was so much hurt. The light hurt where it reached us through the trees, us creatures in the water, kicking and crying and flapping like mad. I reached – I did reach. My fingers closed around a thrashing body. I held on.

It started to rain. The rain fell so hard on the surface of the pond it seemed to fall up. The body in my hands thrashed. It twisted, it kicked. The rain pelted down as the sun rose. I tipped my head back, my mouth open. The rain poured in. And I let go.

The duck shook just the once, then swam pleasantly off.

I swam to the bank. I sat down beside my boots. The rain stopped. The day showed up. It came quickly all at once, like it does every day if you're watching it come. I would sit where I was, I decided, right there next to my clothes and my boots. I would wait for them to dry, that's what I would do. I was an adult and these were my boots. No one could stop me.

Cleaning Products

Claudia was taking the coffee pot off the stove and preparing to rinse it when Annie's phone rang. She held the handle of the pot with one hand and took a hold of the bottom, to unscrew it. The metal was too hot. She swore and dropped the pot into the sink.

'It's him,' Annie said, holding up the phone.

Claudia turned on the tap and pushed both her hands under the cold.

'Don't you,' Claudia said. 'It's two days to go. Don't you.'

'Okay,' Annie said, laying the phone on the bench. 'It's all right. Easy, easy.'

The ringing stopped. For a moment there was only the sound of water rushing, then it started up again.

'It's okay,' Annie said. 'It could be some emergency. I'm putting him on speaker. It's okay.'

'Oh my god Mum. She's got a tail, I swear to god.'

He had been a little boy with sausages for toes who cried in the winter because he did not like to wear long-sleeved pyjamas. Now his voice filled the house, pushing everything further out towards the walls.

'She totally thinks she's a mermaid, no joke. I said, but are you saying you want to be a mermaid or you wish you were a mermaid or are trying to be a mermaid or like what?'

'Nicholas,' Annie said. 'What are you saying, is something wrong?'

Claudia picked up a tea towel and began, slowly, to dry her hands. She closed her eyes. When she opened them again the kitchen window showed through to the summer dark which was threatening to descend; it was taking such a long time to do it. In the paperbark trees, cicadas screamed.

'Nicholas,' Annie said. 'What are you talking about?'

'Oh my god, Mum, now she's holding her breath. She's not coming up. She's trying to prove something to me personally. She's gonna kill herself.'

Claudia hung the tea towel on the sink and moved into the living room. She sat down on the lounge beside the old cat whose eyes curled with blue smoke like two marbles in her head.

'Nicholas,' Annie said, 'it's better I hang up. If there's an emergency you know you can call. But this doesn't count. That's the rules.'

'Is Mimi there too? Mum? Mim? Am I on speaker?'

Claudia scratched the cat behind her good ear. The other ear had a large lump inside it which was a deep shade of purple in a certain light. The vet said at this stage they should let the lump go.

'Yes Nicholas,' Claudia said. 'I'm here. Mum is here.'

'Oh my god,' he said. 'I've so missed your voice.'

The cat jumped off the lounge and went out of the room. She was all bones and matted fur but still, now and then, certain things occurred to her.

'I'm sorry for the texts. I love you Mimi.'

As the cat went down the back steps, the light in the middle of the garden came on. The globe cast a soft milky glow over the lawn. Narrowly missing the light was the Hills Hoist and the rotting fence. They shared this fence with an old woman who had left a bromeliad on their front porch when it was clear to everyone he was finally gone.

'I'm close this time, I was just thinking you could help. Cleaning stuff for the inspection. It's tomorrow morning.'

Claudia sat forward and rubbed her hands over her knees.

'Why aren't you buying cleaning products?' she said. 'That's included in your budget each week.'

'You spent all of it on fluids,' Annie said. 'Is that what you're telling me?'

'I just need some cleaning stuff, like sponges. Like bleach.'

'If you're meant to be preparing for your inspection,' Annie said, 'then that's what you're meant to be doing. Where are you?'

'I would really appreciate you doing this for me. I would really appreciate it, you guys. I'm reaching out.'

The cat made her way in a broken rhythm across the lawn. All her life she'd been smart as a hat – pausing with disdain at every shift in the grass, a paw suspended in the air at every sound in the street – but now she moved like a wooden toy a child makes at school.

'We'll get some cleaning products,' Claudia said. 'We'll bring them around.'

'I'm hanging up now,' Annie said.

'Mum.'

'I'm hanging up, now. I'm hanging up.'

Annie picked up the keys. Claudia locked the doors. Annie backed the car out of the driveway. Claudia turned the radio up. They both felt the soft bump. Annie stopped the car, and they climbed out.

The cat's mouth was open and there was blood on her teeth.

'Oh my God,' Claudia said. 'Why's she screaming like that?'

Annie got down on her knees and slipped her hands under the cat. She was careful with the head, which was too loose on the neck. Claudia just stood there, tall as a house.

'Come on,' Annie said. 'You have to drive. It's all right.'

At the vet they sat together on plastic chairs. There were three blow-up fleas hanging from the ceiling, which knocked against one another every time someone opened the door. When the vet appeared they both stood up.

'We've given her some pain relief,' the vet said. 'She's a bit more stable now.'

'Will she be okay?' Claudia said.

'Why don't you come through.'

The cat was arranged perfectly inside the oxygen cell with her head on her front legs. The cell was on a long, steel table in the middle of a room lined with cages. Some of the cages were open but everyone inside them was quiet like they knew where they were and how they ought to behave.

'Take your time,' the vet said. 'You can unzip it if you like.'

Annie took a hold of the zip and opened the flap. Claudia put her hand through and stroked the cat's head.

'She's not in any pain,' the vet said. 'That's the important thing.'

A girl appeared with a clipboard, which she held out for the vet. Claudia took in the round face of the girl, the large earrings, the shaved head.

'Do we have a decision to make,' she said. 'Is this why we're here?'

'It's very hard,' the vet said, holding the clipboard to her chest. Then she held it out.

'No rush,' she said. 'Take your time.'

Claudia took the clipboard. Annie closed the zip.

'There are options,' Claudia said. 'What are our options here?'

'Come on,' Annie said. 'Sweetheart.'

The phone rang again as they were getting in the car. They sat there and listened to their son without interrupting him.

He was at a pool party. He'd had two tinnies of light beer, three at the most. He wasn't drunk. The inspection was real. The mermaid was also true – even though it was so unbelievable. He was sorry. The place was filthy and if he was going to be honest he had to admit he had bought nothing in the way of cleaning products even though he needed them, badly. And the mould was a serious problem. He had a plan to fix the mould with bleach and, after it dried, with good quality paint.

'But I've used the four-twenty,' he said. 'I don't really know how. Not on fluids. I haven't bought anything myself.'

'Nicholas,' Claudia said, taking out her phone. 'Nicholas, we're going now to pick up some cleaning products and then we're going to your place, to clean up. We'll do it.'

'Mim.'

'I'm transferring one hundred dollars,' she said. 'I'm doing it now, mate. Okay. It's done.'

'I'm going to hang up now,' Annie said.

'Mum.'

'I'm hanging up, mate. I'm hanging up.'

Annie turned the key in the ignition and got the headlights on and backed out of the parking lot. Claudia sat holding her phone in both hands, looking out the window. On the highway cars swept in and out of the dark, blinking red, yellow, white. They all had a certain rhythm about them which showed they weren't entirely separated in time and space but which nevertheless moved them individually. As Annie pulled into the parking lot outside the supermarket a song came on the radio they both knew by heart. Annie reached for Claudia. She kissed her temple. She touched her face. They stayed in the car with their seatbelts on until the song disappeared, indefatigably, into the next.

Jack and Juliana

Cats! That apartment had cats. They didn't live inside his mother's apartment – they lived outside and fought themselves like wild. They were the kind of cats who'd lose track of whose back leg was whose and wouldn't stop gnawing through until they tasted bone and ran away. Juliana was standing at the window looking down.

'The guy across the road feeds them,' Jack said.

He was lying on the bed in his mother's apartment thinking that, everything aside, the whole university thing was working out fine. Maybe it was working out better than he'd hoped because things were happening so fast and he was really living, he could feel that now, life was happening all around him and he was inside of that life and it had its own special momentum he'd never felt before. He put his hand under his head and considered the bare back of Juliana.

'What do you mean he feeds them?' she said.

He rolled over and got up, pulling the bed sheet off with him. Then he changed his mind and got rid of the sheet. He stood beside her at the window.

'He's a hoarder,' Jack said.

Down on the street was a small cat standing next to a bin. The cat took a few steps sideways and then stood still again.

'If he feeds them,' she said, 'that makes them his.'

'They're not his cats,' he said. 'They're nobody's cats.'

Jack turned to Juliana. He thought he must look especially beautiful in the moonlight through the window and without making too much of it he took a slower, deeper breath. He felt a power inside himself he had been feeling lately. Her breasts, he thought, it was to do with her breasts.

'My god,' he said, reaching out.

The night was right there at the backs of his ears and he was in it and he loved it and he thought, this is what it is.

'It's sad for the cats,' Juliana said.

Jack kissed her neck. He put his hand between her legs.

'Oh my god,' she said.

'Oh god,' he said.

'Oh my god,' she said. 'Jack. I think that cat is dead.'

But he couldn't hear anything, he was so absorbed in himself. He was loving her but he was also right inside himself for the first time. For the first time in his life he had this sense of his own mass and it gave him this hot chill down the backs of his legs.

'Jack,' she said. 'Jack. I think that cat is dead. Look.'

He looked out into the night. It was only an empty street.

'They're nobody's cats,' he said. 'Juliana. Oh my god.'

'I'm going down,' she said, pulling away and going out.

Jack sat down on the bed. He opened a beer. He would wait here, he knew that. For as long as it took her out there on the street he would sit here, on his mother's bed, not doing anything.

'Look,' Juliana said, coming back in.

Jack looked at the cat. It was so small in her hands. It looked smaller still when it kicked its ugly legs. It did this just the once. Juliana sat down on the bed.

'It's not dead yet,' she said.

Jack put his hand on her leg. He understood this was love. This was all that it meant. He decided if they married he'd have her change her hair, but apart from that he wouldn't change anything.

The Nature of Ghosts

My ancestors are doing this thing where they turn my oven on. I wake up every night to this uncanny glow. I stand in the doorway of the kitchen staring at the oven – all red and puffed up and roaring with nothing inside itself to attach its heat to.

I lie back down on my bed, just accepting the glow. And because my ancestors have nothing better to do than to fuck with my oven and criticise me they stand around the flat, all crowded in and superficially solemn while I weep like this is some funeral.

I hear brushstrokes between them.

'What are we going to *do* with her?'

One grandmother or other takes my hair out and strokes it. Another fits herself easily between the bedhead and the pillow and soothes me by running her cool ghostly hand over my forehead, my face. I appreciate this. Understand that in life these women had not cared for me a drip – some of them hadn't even bothered to be alive – but they have more time in the after-life to reflect and more capacity to be available, if not exactly physically or emotionally, then at least spiritually.

'It's like she does not *care* for fire safety,' one of them says.

I don't know any of their names and we don't address one another directly. They are all the different versions of everything we are. One of them is missing an eye. Another an arm. One of them appears as a baby in a glass jar and I feel she is infinitely more regal than the rest, the way she positions herself in the amber liquid near the spider's web above the blinds. She is the one who really makes it clear to me that the woman I love is not going to call and that at this late stage it is really over between us.

'Oh, yeah,' the baby says. 'Done, sugar. All done.'

And then I lose sight of her because a whole bunch of ancestors swarm onto my bed, piling one on top of the other, smelling like myself and of the morning, getting all comfortable, slipping in and out of each other in their commotion. Then they settle in to watch a program about bees on a gigantic television screen that has just appeared where the window used to be.

Somebody is making popcorn. Somebody else puts a hand on my leg and I think it is my ancestor in the jar but then I realise this is not possible.

I finally email the real estate agent and describe the issue. The oven is turning on in the middle of the night – I believe this may be a fire hazard? I am vaguely concerned he will not believe me. In any case he writes back. He says a man will appear.

The man when he shows up is young and small enough to fit into places but he can't work out what's wrong.

'How actually old is this oven?' I say. 'That's what I want to know.'

'Not that old,' the man says. 'Not old at all.'

He turns the dial back and forth. He pulls the oven out.

'Oh god,' I say. 'Is it so gross back there?'

'It's not too bad,' he says. 'But I can't fix it today. I'll just turn it off. Where's the plug for this thing?'

'I don't know,' I say.

'There isn't a plug. Where's the fuse box?'

'Not in there,' I say, as he opens and closes doors.

Pretty soon there is nothing left to open and close so he goes under the building and locates it there.

Later the woman calls.

'We've got an oven for you.'

'An oven!' I say.

I express my surprise.

'We quoted the landlord for replacement and repair,' the woman says.

She seems tired, so tired that she doesn't even bother to finish her lines. It is okay because I fill them in for her.

'They chose replacement,' I say.

'Yes.'

I know as she says it she is so tired of these calls – these calls across generations of women all in lines for heat, all barefoot, all hungry, all holding hands. My grandmother and her mother and her mother among them, going all the way back until everybody is so black there is no question at all. I know this woman is so tired making phone call after phone call on behalf of women and history and tenancy rights everywhere. In my head she has a semi-permanent set of auburn curls. I love her drastically but I do not know her name.

Something like Sheryl.

And then I remember, sickening, that was the name of my first teddy bear. Why Sheryl?

The smell of the damp fur that isn't real comes rushing in. Also yellow soap and shredded cereal, thick and sour with hot skimmed milk and bananas chopped up inside with the skin on.

'We can deliver it tomorrow,' the woman says. 'Between seven and eight.'

'All right,' I say. 'Thank you.'

The next day I get up early. I think of the oven that is coming to me and of everything that is going to happen to me in my life, all of the surprises that will enter my life and make my life worth living and that will prolong my life. Then I think I better prepare the place for guests.

I put away the clothes and put the line away. I make the bed. I wash up the dishes and put them in the rack. Everything I do has this tone to it that says, I don't live like this. I get myself dressed and sit down on the bed.

Before me, time falls away. I know exactly how the groom feels waiting for his bride. I think of mine in the truck, all white and square, all cold and stiff because she's never been opened before.

I do not mind the waiting. Then suddenly I do. I do a shocking thing. I walk down the aisle without any hesitation, past all the guests, agog, I simply walk like this out of the church and into the rainy, winter day. I have to get cream. All of a merry sudden I have to get cream for the coffee I will need later on.

But then I see her emerging from the truck. A man is helping her. She is turned away from me so I can't see her face but I tell you I stop. I stand there in the rain just looking at her. She looks incredibly wide and vulnerable, out there on the street.

I hurry back inside and answer the door like a normal person. I sit on the bed, all normal, while the installation occurs. At one point one of the men asks me if I want to keep the old muffin trays. He holds up a muffin tray.

'You don't make muffins,' he says.

'That's true,' I say.

The other guy thrusts the manual into my hands, and they leave.

I open the manual. I read about the test cake with my eyebrows somewhat raised. I read about her three button programmable clock. I read the general hints and tips section which shows me, with pictures, exactly how to handle her.

Using both hands, gently remove the inner glass by slipping it out and lifting it with care away from the door.

Hand wash only with warm water, soap and a soft cloth. Wipe inner and outer flaps gently.

Open the door fully to access the hinges then rotate the stirrups on both hinges fully towards the door.

To release the top trim, press the ribbed clip until the stirrups draw back.

Care should be taken not to damage other parts.

I shut the manual. I put it on the bench.

'Oh no,' I say. I cannot deal with this.

I take a shower and lie face down on the bed. I set my hair on a towel and I try to fall asleep. Of course, in the daylight, the ancestors are gone. Having finished their legitimate business with me they have moved off without any fanfare towards the next place as if my life, my rental flat, my completely broken heart and my relationship with my kitchen appliances are all one big joke. But that is the nature of ghosts.

The surprise is I can feel her waiting with my ears. All shiny white and cool, incredibly clean, but waiting nonetheless. Waiting just where she is to come roaring to life.

Sea Creatures (Goodbye, with all my Love)

I

My little brother came into my bedroom all high. This in the house we grew up in, with the Jacaranda tree. I could look out my window all the way to the city. My brother came in and I was alone. This was my childhood bedroom. The bed, covered in lilac and green petals, was by the window, but there was this space in between where my brother often hid to scare me at night. Hiding and scaring – this was our thing, when we were kids. There was this one night I remember where he tried to save me. He had stood behind the curtains, between the window and my bed, planning to jump out when I was doing my homework or putting away my clothes. But instead of coming into my bedroom like normal, switching on the light and mucking around, I hopped straight into bed so he stood there, in the dark. He knew he would scare me too much, it was going too far, so he tried to creep out of my room once he thought I was asleep. I was not asleep and I screamed and I screamed. And he screamed and we laughed and we laughed and we laughed because he was pinned up against the curtains so sorry, for the scream, and trying to stop me.

II

My brother came into my bedroom all high and I knew he was high and I told this to him because this was my room. We were a middle class family and this was my room. I had chosen the aqua walls myself, to speak of the sea, and the violet finishings were a gesture towards femininity even though, by that stage, I was convinced I was turning into a man. I was writing about breasts in my diary and such, my brother's best friend's sister's big breasts. Clarissa was her name. Clarissa had big, beautiful breasts. I wrote of them in my diary and cancelled them out with the same pen. So my brother came in, pinned to the hilt, and I was angry with him. You're so high, I said. He got into my bed but I rolled him. I got one leg either side and got my hands around his neck.

I knew he was injecting into his eyeballs by that time. I might have killed him myself if my father hadn't come in and chastised me. He's all high, I said. But he acted like I was doing this terrible thing. He's high, I said. He might die, I said. You better watch him. My father said, you watch yourself. You're skating on thin ice, he said. My brother heard nothing. If he did, he didn't say. I left him in the dark, in that place we had played in before, with the little girl trimmings and the nice lace curtains that moved on the surface of the glass and showed through to the purple leaves out the front. There were the buildings at the end of the street, tiny buildings that blinked, mocking me, but which I knew I would get to, I would get out, in the end. Meanwhile my little brother all high in my bed, pumped up under his quiet, pale skin, his blue veins running every way. When I came back, hoping he might be asleep, he actually was injecting into his eyeball. Now I never liked my father. I never liked him any more than my little brother did, but just then I knew my father was the solution to this. So I let out a scream to call him to this and my little brother with his big, white fuelled body, he screamed back at me and as we stood there in my room, screaming, his eye began to bleed.

III

The needle was orange along the trunk, and I thought of snow. The needle was a carrot off a man's face lying in the snow of the unmade bed. It was just a little blood at first, a lively tear, all pumped up and convinced of itself. I stood in the doorway of my bedroom and I screamed and my little brother screamed and then his eye really, really began to bleed.

IV

We stood there screaming, him bleeding, and the quality of his scream took on a different note. I was determined for my father to come, to take care of this. This was his direct business! I was determined for the windows to burst open in that sick place and to let us all breathe, breathe, but a sudden change occurred, in the nature of my brother's scream. This is an interesting story I have for you here to do with the nature, the texture of a scream.

V

He was frightened now, there was so much blood on his face, streaming now, from his pretty amber eye which I'd known better than my own eye all my life because he was my little brother and oh, I loved him so. But I was frightening him. I was frightening him so that my father would come in and I was frightening him with something deeper, and he let me know this with his scream. As he screamed the blood gushed down his face. It really did. I was a real live witness to this and what I witnessed in this moment between us was that he needed me to soothe him. It took me a moment to actually realise that while his life really was in danger, and we required an actual adult to help, he was afraid of the solution, of what the solution might mean, and this made the screaming different and the bleeding worse and he was afraid of something else, something far beyond death, something far beyond the blood all over his face, his bare chest, and now, so much blood, darkening in a small patch at the waist of his Daffy Duck boxer shorts. God, this was so the nineties. And I stopped screaming. I put my arms around him. I put my face to his bare, white, bloody chest because I understood then that to hold him in this single moment in his life was more important than his life. So, yes, I did this. And our father did not come.

VI

The house was silent and we stood barefoot in that room. The carpet was a little wet from all the blood and the screams. It was like how sea creatures disturb the sand into mud for a moment and then it settles once they are gone. It settled. The carpet was a little wet from all of the blood because something had gone wrong regarding the needle in his eye and he would/would not go blind but we were not there yet. For the moment we were simply two beating hearts standing there in that room and that was everything. For the moment I knew just what I had to do and I did it with all my love. I did it willingly.

Flight

Ted was in love with Susie. It was summer. Ted was nine and Susie was twelve. They were in the same fourth-grade class because Susie had started school three years late.

'Slow down,' Susie said. 'Faster than that.'

Ted was walking her home. He knew he was in love with her. Everywhere he knew this. He knew that he'd feel it for the rest of his life. More than that he knew what to do with his love.

'Stop here,' Susie said.

Ted stopped.

'Wait,' Susie said.

Ted waited.

'Something's coming,' Susie said. 'Any minute now.'

The heat filled Ted's eyes. His school shirt stuck to him.

'What is it?' he said.

'Shh,' Susie said.

Ted looked down at her. He sniffed the top of her head. She had caught him doing this once before. Are you smelling my head? she had said. That is so weird. Now he was more careful when he did this. He was careful with everything – he had learned to be this. In his love for Susie he had learned many things. For example, he no longer asked to pat her little bump. Instead, he patiently waited for her to ask him. It might be a long time between pats, but then it would come. Her voice low and sweet, when they were alone at her place, or alone at school in the corner of the library on the beanbags surrounded by non-fiction books. Can you pat me? she would whisper. His eager heart would shout. Then she would lean forward and he would lift up her shirt, exposing the fatty mass on her back above the band of her shorts. He would reach out, touch it gently with the tips of his fingers – growing braver, older, every moment, loving her like this.

Presently, the sound of a motorbike engine came to them. Then it appeared.

They watched as it roared along the quiet, empty street. They watched it turn the corner and vanish. Susie tipped her head up and looked Ted in the face.

'Exactly,' she said, her eyes shining. 'I am essentially travelling into the future with my intelligence,' she said. 'In a single moment I gather all of the possibilities, no matter how remote…' She cupped the fingers of one hand to make the shape of a bowl, and moved the fingers of the other in a flurry on top. 'And whoosh – then I get it.' She blew her fingers apart. 'The one vision left.'

Ted nodded. There were beads of perspiration on her upper lip, which he wanted to remove with the tip of his tongue. He was hit by this thought as if it were a stick.

'Onward Christian soldiers,' Susie said, stabbing her finger straight ahead. 'We're going for level nine, today. And a pink doughnut.'

When they reached the shops, Ted pushed Susie towards the bakery.

'Stop,' Susie said. 'I have to fix my hair.'

She took out her hairband. She shook her blonde mane.

'How do I look?'

'Okay,' Ted said.

'Ted.'

Ted closed his eyes.

'You look like the devil in disguise as a woman of the night.'

'Thank you,' Susie said. 'Okay. Let's go.'

At the bakery the bell dinged when Ted pushed Susie through the door.

'You're late,' the owner said, coming out from the back. She put her hands on her hips. 'What will it be?'

'A pink doughnut,' Susie said.

The owner put the doughnut in a bag and came around the front. She dangled it in front of Susie.

'And what do you have for me?'

Ted opened Susie's school bag and brought out a blue manila folder. He handed it to Susie, who opened it.

'This is something special,' she said, taking out a small square of paper. 'It took more than a week. I call it Solar Plex. It's a graphic representation of my emotional state pre and post birth, but as seen from outer space.'

The owner took the drawing and considered it. On a black background a white circle glowed.

'Ah,' she said. 'This is the moon, is it?'

'Oh my god,' Susie said. 'I am so not that way inclined. But if you observe it alongside the others I think you will see a kind of spiritual progression which is planetary in scale. So in a word, yes.'

The owner pinned the square on a corkboard next to Susie's other squares. Then she stood back.

'Yes, I see it,' she said.

'Me too,' Ted said.

'Hey,' Susie said. 'I don't see it.' She shrugged. 'But that's art.'

'And when are you off?' the owner said.

'Are you joking?' Susie said. 'I've completely changed my mind. In China, you know what children do when they lose a tooth? They throw it on the roof of their house for good luck. And what do we do? We sell it for a buck. Put it under a pillow and sell it to a fairy for a buck. They need me on earth. I'm not going anywhere.'

Ted shook his head.

'See you next week,' the owner said.

While Susie ate her doughnut, Ted climbed the tower. She held the doughnut with one hand and flapped the other in the air, directing wildly.

'To the left!' she shouted. 'No, no! The other left!'

Ted gripped the rope so tight it burned. With the tips of his toes he reached through the air for the next piece of rope, the next landing place.

'Yes! Yes!' Susie shouted.

Ted found the rope. He shifted his weight. Then he looked up, reached out, and hauled himself through space.

'Level nine!' Susie shouted. 'Now you can fly!'

Ted gripped the rope. The heat throbbed in his ears.

'It's level nine! Turn around!'

Ted twisted his head. He looked down at her. She was so small down there, just a tiny head and tiny hands, furious, waving at him from a chair. The children were swarming like bugs. He did not know how to fly. Ted opened his mouth but no air came in. He opened and closed his mouth. Where was the air?

'Ted!' Susie shouted.

From that great height her voice reached him. He who was now taller than the trees and capable, in his love, of just about any physical feat.

'Let's go!' Susie shouted. 'Okay! Now! Fly!'

He gripped the rope tighter and squeezed his eyes shut against the flight.

Monster

Right around the time the dog started barking at the fence I started seeing this monster every time I closed my eyes. Pretty soon the monster was there even with my eyes open. I had an idea of how the monster looked but I couldn't put words to it, myself. More than anything it was a feeling, and the feeling took over me. It occurred under the skin, around the bones of my jaw and up high on the sides of my head. It was a feeling of something growing, that's what I'm saying it was. But he was also completely individual, the monster, in and of himself, and in a way I didn't have anything to do with him.

This was all around the time I lost my last job. It was hot but there were full moons four days in a row. Now I don't put anything down to magic, I'm not that way at all, but that moonlight was so bright you could take a piece of paper out on your back steps at three o'clock in the morning and read from it. The dog was the one person I had going in my life. She was entirely reliable and didn't have an opinion on anything. She wasn't my dog but she acted like she was. I fed and watered her. By the time the monster came along the dog was nearly dead, but she kept doing this thing where she'd invent a new life. For example, she'd never said a word in her life and then she started barking like crazy at the fence near the lantana which grew like a demented pink and yellow beast. Traditionally she never did spend much time in the yard but now it seemed there was plenty for her out there and then she started barking at the fence, just like that. I decided that was death at the fence and I liked her tone. But then I saw that her front leg was stuck in the lantana. I released her. She was quiet in my arms with her arms all limp in front and her tired head, quiet and closed and leaning on my chest. If I'd have stayed that way she would have fallen asleep.

The day I lost my job it was 42 degrees. I'd done nine trips to the tip in six hours. Rafters, mainly. Down three flights of stairs. Load them in the truck. Get up the stairs in leaps and bounds because Felix was watching me. Don't let me say a thing about Felix, the way he watches. That bastard. I swear to god he'll be pulling a ceiling out one panel at a time, at the top of a 40-step ladder, and he'll scream at you to leave the cake alone. Baklava. His wife brings it on a tray. She goes to all this trouble to do it up with cellophane and you fall in love with her in 14 seconds flat. She's about sixty years old but pretty as fucking hell. I was hoping to get her on her own. I thought I could do something – I was in that kind of state. She was on her way up to Felix with this plate of flatbread cut into triangles and she stopped where I was, right beside the ute. I was arranging rafters in the back when she came. I wished, as she stood there saying something to me, I was doing something much more impressive. I wished my arms were covered in streaks of blood where the nails had gotten caught, or else that I had some serious tattoos. Felix is a short, round guy about sixty himself but he has all these serious tattoos.

See things were looking different but I won't go into that. And I tried something on. Right there outside the hardware store I leaned in and put one hand to the back of her long neck. She saw me coming and stepped back. She said something and then she was gone, disappeared into that chemical street, then suddenly it was near dusk and I was sitting there at her house, on her couch, with Felix beside me saying how it was. That if I didn't get some professional help he'd have to let me go – job and all. What do you mean by that? I said. What do you mean by this term, job and all? I was drunk and I thought I was sharp, onto things. I thought, it is just like Felix to go at me this way. He repeated his offer to get me some help and I said I'd think about it but I guessed I wouldn't do it. I was thinking more seriously about drinking just then and when Felix dropped me home I went inside, waited several minutes, then went out again.

The Ezy Bottle-O is at the top of my street. It probably isn't quite that close but it seems that way to me. The old bloke who works at the Ezy Bottle-O reminds me of my father. Now he is a guy who died a long time ago. A big asshole. My grandfather was an asshole before him, I come from a long line of them. I was being a total asshole when I went in there that day. I was well off my face and I'd made a pass at my boss's old lady and I had this dream up front in my mind that I just couldn't leave alone. In the dream I lived in a tiny room with two windows and I lay down to sleep and I was feeling so good. I was drifting off to sleep. Next thing I know there are birds streaming fast and black out both windows. Six thousand birds flapping. Hitting the window, too. Scrambling to get into the room which they could, easily, because the window was open. It was one you pull up, open a bit at the bottom, and all these birds started coming in, butting their heads and coming in sideways, crawling under to get in the room and scratching their way through. They were big black birds with hooked over black beaks. They used their claws to get in, there was the sound of them doing this, but they also used their hot little heads to push their way through. The dog was there, in the dream. I took up the dog. I took up the dog and opened the door for outside and went outside where I'd be safe but the birds were all there, I was knocked sideways by birds. There was nowhere to return, my room was crawling with them, and I stood in front of the fridge in the Ezy Bottle-O, somewhat paralysed. Frankly I was looking for something to shut me all the way down but the end of it was that I didn't have a choice. Those birds will return, I thought. Either way they'll come back. I got a six-pack of dark beer and a bottle of sparkling wine. At the counter the old bloke said, you want a carry bag? I was being this asshole so I said, I certainly do. I'm going to have to double bag this, he said. And I said just like this big asshole, do whatever you need to do, old man. Do whatever you need to do.

Well you have to understand I'd had some run-ins with this guy. For one thing he never remembered me. He just refused. I'd had a few conversations with him about his dog. He loved his dog. And then this one time I went in and he refused to sell me rum. I'd just brought my keys and the cash out with me. He said, if you look under twenty-five I'm required by law to ask you for ID. I was panicking, I needed rum. I said, I'm thirty-three years old for god's sake – I'm always here. He wouldn't budge. And then the dog occurred to me and I put that to him. Hey remember the dog? I said. I came in that day with my dog and you told me about your dog. Remember? And the old man looked at me for some lonely time. Right, he said snapping his fingers at me. Yes, I remember you now.

And so I was standing there waiting to pay and this had all just occurred to me again and the old bloke was double-bagging the beer and I thought to rub it in, what a jerk he had been. So how's the dog? I said. How is the dog, old man? I put the emphasis on is and also on old. I might also have leaned my elbow on the counter. I might even have turned my head and considered the customer behind me. Maybe I winked. Anyway the old man put the wine in a brown bag and twisted the top. He put that in the bags with the beer and he said, I had to get him done. Monday. He's gone. The customer behind me wore a blue t-shirt. This fact doesn't make any difference but it's part of the story.

I paid on my credit card and got out of there fast. I got home and put the beers in the freezer because I like them very cold. I opened the bottle of sparkling wine. Normally I wouldn't work it that way but just then I couldn't feel anything. I was looking for something to take me all the way down, even past where I couldn't feel anything, to the quiet. It didn't come. Something came. For instance, when the wine kicked in I lit the candles to keep the mosquitoes away and it occurred to me how hot the metal was. I turned up my palm. I pressed the torch into the inside of my left forearm a couple of neat times. When I was finished I admired the two round, perfect circles burned into the skin. They were extremely symmetrical circles and I thought if someone came along and wanted to know which circle I liked best, I couldn't choose. It was impossible to choose, I realised. I liked both circles evenly.

I could hear the dog coughing up out the back. Perhaps she'd been doing that for some time. Anyway I went out there. She was sitting in front of the bed making this obvious back and forth motion with her head. I studied her some more, like she was a stranger. She was small and white but apart from that I didn't know anything about her. If she had coughed like this before, for instance, I honestly had no idea. Perhaps she had reverse hiccups. Anyway she continued coughing in this way and then she spat something up. I went closer to see what she'd spat up on the floor, expecting it to be a tiny black bird. I was dizzy and drunk and there were black birds on my brain but then I saw what it was. It was only a small, clear puddle of silly foam. I looked from the foam to the dog. Her eyes were so grey. Then she moved across the room and curled up in her bed and I knew if I sat there any longer she'd die right in front of me. I grabbed my keys and the bottle and went out.

It was an ordinary night, another full moon, and there wasn't anything to live for, I didn't think. But somewhere in there it was crucial to walk. I thought I'd feel better if I was moving and it turned out I was right. I drank from the bottle and moved with purpose. I only stopped at the park because of what was taking place there on the path.

The path went in a loop around the park. There was a pony on the path. There was a man attached to the pony, who was riding a bike. At first I thought the pony was a dog. It was dark and I didn't have my glasses on. I've seen big dogs before.

The pony was moving at a steady pace. I looked around for someone else to see it. There was nobody. The pony was coming around the curve. It was coming at a pace and was now almost right alongside me. I had to say something. I said, wow, a pony! And that's when I saw how old the man was. He was like my old man but he was different somehow. He wore a helmet. It was new and white. He had this severe look on his face and he rode like that too, with his knees about his chin. The pony was tethered to him, the rope was around his wrist. I repeated the wow. The old man ignored me. Either that or he didn't hear. He didn't look in my direction and then he was gone, working those pedals like crazy, gone with his pony towards the other end of the park where he made a left and sharply pulled the pony around. The pony put its head down and the old man yanked on the rope. Keep your head up! the old man shouted. Keep your head up you stupid thing!

I stood there and watched this happen several times. I was drunk and I had the feeling something big was coming on. The old man pedalled like crazy and the pony moved beside him in a trot. The problem always came at the top of the hill, right before the descent, there was this terrible beat when the old man yanked hard on the rope and the pony put down its head and the old man worked those pedals hard. Keep your head up! he shouted. Keep your head up, you stupid thing! His legs never stopped going around and I could have stood there and watched the whole thing happen over and over and over again. Instead I turned back for home and I started to run. I was running from something I couldn't see in the dark. I was in trouble, I knew that.

I woke up the following day in the hospital, asking for my brother. I had the most unbelievable headache from where I'd passed out on the street. I woke up with a nurse standing over me who had pink lipstick on and bracelets which jangled and an Adam's apple that judged me for wasting everybody's time. I got off the bed, my head blinding me, and walked home. I had to sort myself out. I explained to myself things had gone a bit far this time, I would have to wind it back, I would stop drinking for a week and see how I was after that and if I was doing much better I'd never drink again. Or I'd drink, but moderately. I'd start up rowing again. I would have a conversation with Felix and get my job back — I'd apologise for everything and be completely sincere. After that was done I'd keep my big mouth firmly shut. Maybe I'd even see about a doctor, like Felix said. I would change, I was absolutely committed to this and, if I couldn't change, I would pretend to change and that would be the same thing. I felt good, in a sense. I had a look at the time. I thought a little beer just now would settle things, put a stamp on my big decision. It was quiet in the house. Quiet, and not yet time for lunch.

The dog was lying in the middle of the kitchen floor. She produced a noise and I had to step over her to get to the freezer. I took a beer out and put it in the sink. I filled a glass with water and sat down to wait. I had the feeling things were going down fast. I sipped at the water and lay down on the lounge and next thing I know I have a tickle up my nose. I put the tips of my index and middle fingers to my right nostril and blow, gently. The gently is important. I can feel the shape of the thing coming out my left nostril. It has feathers and is curled in a ball and the more I blow the more it comes out. Unfurling. It falls on my left shoulder. And I lie there unable to move and thinking I should open my eyes, reach up my hand, turn on the light to see what is there. Is it possible I've just blown one of those baby birds out my nose? I was thinking this way. Then I woke up. The dog came to me slowly, slowly. Then quickly, all at once.

She was still in the kitchen. Both her eyes were closed and they fluttered now and then but there was a fairly long time between the flutters. The tip of her tongue was hanging out the side of her mouth. It was grey. I lifted her up. She was stunningly light in my arms. I tried to think if she had been so light the day before, when I had lifted her out of the lantana.

I put the dog in a green bag and took her on the bus. She lay at the bottom of the bag, puffing. I kept my eyes on the driver and I let the dog's head come out. She kept her eyes open that entire bus ride, and I noticed for the first time how long her white eyelashes were.

At the vet they were an hour away from doing consultations but when the receptionist saw the dog she slid the window closed and opened the door. I put the bag on the floor. It was a nice office with a wooden table in the middle. On the mantelpiece were books about dogs and there were pictures of dogs on the wall. Everything smelled sweet and hairy, like dogs. There was a statue of the insides of a dog's heart on the desk. I looked down at the dog. Soon the vet appeared. He looked about nineteen. He looked like a movie star and I told this to him. He smiled at me. He asked for the dog and I lifted her up. I set her down on the table between us. The vet inspected her and then sat down behind the desk.

'There's fluid on the lungs,' he said. 'We could put her in an oxygen tank and see how she goes overnight.'

'How much is that?' I said.

'About twelve hundred for the night. It might give her a few days, a week at the most. The other option is to euthanize.'

We both looked at the dog. She puffed quietly. I tried to think if I felt anything for the dog. It hadn't occurred to me how stinking she was, perhaps it was the room, but something stank so much it was hard to take a breath. I thought of the old man, of the asshole I had been.

'Okay,' I said. 'She's old anyway.'

'There are forms,' the vet said. 'You'll have to sign these first.'

'How long will it take?'

'Not long,' the vet said.

I signed the forms and gave them back. The vet took her out of the room to get her prepared. He brought her back in a white towel. Her arm was shaved and there was a tube in her nose. I laughed.

'Do you want to hold her?' he said.

I didn't know that I did.

'She's not my dog,' I said. 'I haven't had her for long.'

The vet laid the dog on the table. He spread his big movie star hand over her head and started to pat her, crooning softly. Then he took up the syringe. The fluid in the syringe was bright blue and I sat forward in the chair because I was looking at that bright blue and thinking of swimming pools. I thought of the pool my father built us when we were kids. He used to put me in a blow-up ring and spin me around and I would look up at the sky and the sky would spin into the camellia tree. My brother, at the edge, would scream and clap his hands.

'Wait,' I said.

The vet stopped. He held one hand firm over the dog's little head.

'All right,' I said. 'She was my brother's dog.'

I sat back in the chair and the vet brought the dog around. I held her, in the rough, white towel. She was taking short, shallow breaths and she was light as a single daisy in my arms. I put my head down close to her head and whispered small things I didn't know, repeatedly. The vet put the needle in and she died.

'I have to check her,' he said.

He pulled up one eyelid and tapped her eyeball with his finger.

'What the fuck?' I said.

'I have to check her reflexes,' he said. 'She's gone.'

I held the dog a little longer. I asked to do this.

'I can give you some time,' the vet said. 'I'll be right back.'

But when he started to leave I couldn't handle that.

'No,' I said. 'No, here you go.'

I handed over the dog.

'I'm sorry,' he said.

I didn't say anything. I went out to reception and paid the bill. It cost ninety-eight dollars. Ninety-eight dollars, to end a little life. I understood just then I had nobody left.

When I stepped outside the sky was hanging low. It was hot. I made it down the steps and onto the grass before I could not go on anymore. I didn't know which way to go. Pretty soon a single fat drop of rain fell like a star exactly where I was on the grass, doubled over myself, the middle gone right out of me. A single stream of spit moved in a line in and out of my mouth as I cried, and the shape of my lips betrayed a terrible hole in my face. I knew I was crying but I could also see it from a distance and I knew I wasn't doing it properly. I was pathetic. My arms hung off my body, hands limp at the end, and then it started to really rain. I watched the water running off my face, finally dragging the spit down all the way. I stood up to go. Someone called out my name. I turned around and he was running down the steps, across the lawn.

'You forgot this,' he said.

He held the collar out.

'Thank you,' I said.

Then he put his arms around me. He held me hard and firm. Then he let me go. He ran back across the lawn and up the stairs in the rain and I walked home.

I started with the monster but I won't quite end that way. The truth is I still cannot see what is there. I sit on my hands and sit on my heart and out the window there is a roof made of brick and something very green, maybe ivy, obscuring in its creeping way most of the brick. I drink from a mug of black tea and say what is possible at the time.

The monster, on the other hand, I say, has an extremely particular look. He is green, with a horn in the middle. Two tails stick out the side of his head. And there are blue and green craters all over his body and face, like warts.

I'd be withholding the truth if I said I'm not scared. I'm not terrified. But I've never known a monster like this one in all my life. And it's here.

A Child's Six

The mother and her two girls were naked in the members' change room of the gymnasium. They had just taken a shower and their three blue towels were hanging on the hooks. Evie was sitting on the wooden bench getting herself dressed. The mother was brushing her hair. Britta was inspecting a pair of the mother's black lace underpants.

'They're a six,' the mother said. 'I'm down to a six.'

She paused to remove a clump of hair from the brush. She let it fall to the floor, then continued brushing.

'Though by now I think I'd be slightly smaller than a six.'

'What size am I?' Britta said.

'You're a six,' the mother said.

'I'm the same size as you?'

'Not a six. A child's six.'

Britta nodded, thinking this through. She hung the underpants on the hook next to the mother's bra, which was also black and trimmed with lace, then tore the paper band off her wrist with her teeth.

'Where do I put this?' she said. 'There's no bin.'

'Just leave it there,' the mother said. 'That's someone's job to clean it up.'

Britta took a towel off the hook and wrapped up her hair, completing this process with an expert flick of the head. Then she sat down. Beside her Evie was eating from a packet of instant noodles. Her t-shirt was long-sleeved and featured an overweight unicorn which was grey, wearing sunglasses and eating a rainbow lollipop. Britta fussed with her smart watch, shaking her head.

'I did 2300 metres,' she said. 'Today.' She looked up. 'I mean 2300 calories.'

'That's impossible,' the mother said, throwing the brush in the bag. 'It's impossible you've done over 2000 on the rower just now. I did nearly 1700 and that was intense. Did you have netball today?'

'We had yoga,' Britta said. 'But we ran around at lunch.'

She stood up, unravelled the towel, and let it fall to the floor. Her dark hair fell in curls around her sharp collarbones.

'Hey,' the mother said. 'That's what the hooks are for.'

Britta was returning the towel to the hook when a woman emerged from the shower cubicle. The woman was dripping wet and fully clothed down to her filthy sandshoes. She held a bag in her large, creamy arms.

'I have no towel,' the woman said. 'Can I borrow a towel?'

Britta turned, her eyes wide. The mother sucked in her breath.

'There are towels at reception,' she said. 'Level Two.'

'Please,' the woman said.

'Reception is upstairs,' the mother said, turning away. 'Level Two.'

The woman turned to face the lockers. She opened a door and slipped her bag inside. Britta grabbed the mother's arm and whispered in her ear. The mother spun around.

'You need a wristband,' she said. 'This is the members' change room. You can't just come in and leave your stuff in here.'

The woman hesitated, then went out. Each step she took she made an awful squelching sound.

'God,' the mother said.

'So gross,' Britta said.

Britta moved across the room to stand in front of the fan. Her lashes were long and dark. Her hazel eyes bulged.

'Guess what I found out today, Mum?' she said.

'What did you find out today, beautiful?'

The mother was applying cream to her face, working it down as far as her neck.

'There is going to be a drop to C's at the next netball game. What if it's me and I don't want to move down? What if it's me? Can I just say no?'

'Sure,' the mother said. 'Evie, want some of this?'

Evie didn't answer. She stared straight ahead. Her hair was still wet and clung to her forehead, releasing cold drops of water so she shivered now and then. She worked at the noodles. Occasionally, her teeth chattered.

'I'll have some,' Britta said, holding out her hand. 'Two people have been dropped but Monique is the worst. It's annoying because she should be the one to go down.'

'Does she know she's the worst?'

'It's pretty obvious.'

'Evie, darling,' the mother said. 'Do you want moisturiser?'

But Evie's gaze was fixed. She ate mechanically.

'Look I don't agree at all,' the mother said, 'with the general approach of the school. I really have a problem with all these special rules. I don't mind saying it, but you've got to do what's fair.'

'What's that?' Evie said. 'In locker 33?'

The foot was an inch high from heel to toe, and a curious shade of blue, but apart from that it was, to anyone observing it, an ordinary foot.

'Oh my god,' the mother said. 'Stay back. Oh my god.'

'It's got toes,' Evie said. 'Also toenails.'

'No,' the mother said.

But Evie was already there.

Britta's hands flapped in space. The mother appeared completely fixed to the spot. Evie moved quickly to see what she could do. She took a towel off the hook and laid it down on the bench. She adjusted it. She placed the baby down in the middle of the towel and started humming as she wrapped him, then brought him to her chest.

The Negotiation

'The rooftop,' she said, like it was obvious.

So we rode the lift to the roof of her hotel.

The day was fine. On the roof a warm wind was blowing. There was a set of sofas, one backed onto the next in the shape of a U, facing the scene. The scene was the entire city laid out in a curve. There were the tops of the houses, the buildings, the churches. The tops of the trees. She sat down on one sofa and I sat down on the next. There was no question regarding this arrangement.

She took off her black, long-sleeved shirt. Her arms, her shoulders, unspeakably fine.

'I haven't felt the sun like this in ages,' she said.

I turned my face to the sun. I closed my eyes against the sun because I could not bear to see the brilliant sky, so fine and blue, over the scene.

'I haven't either,' I said. 'God. It's hot isn't it?'

I did not expect a reply.

'Do you want to talk?' she said.

'Oh, yes,' I said. 'Yes.'

My heart expanded like a stain in my chest.

'So,' I said, using my most grown-up voice. 'So I think it is important, I mean, I want for both of us to be very clear. On what we want in this relationship. I'm as guilty as anyone about saying it, I mean. What I want.' I pushed a finger up under my sunglasses, once into each eye. 'I only want you,' I said, faltering. 'Don't pay attention to this part at all, the tears. They'll come down.'

Her face was so still. All of the skin of her cheeks drew in the direction of her pretty lips. She had her elbow positioned on the back of the sofa and her arm at that angle was most exquisite. I've never known a woman with such arms, such legs. I used to love to lick the backs of those legs. Bite the backs of those ankles, taste the backs of those knees.

We proceeded to list the things that we wanted out of the relationship and it was clear we were on separate pages but we couldn't settle it. And we couldn't end it. Yes, she moved to sit beside me. Yes, she leaned in. Yes, she took my hand and put it up her dress. She was wet and I was wet. She was hot, like her breath. I loved her, this was us.

Later, on the bed, she was calm and relaxed. I lay on top of her, and she ran the tips of her long, cool fingers along my back, down to the waist, and back up again. I had my face in her hair. I kissed her apricot ear and tugged the lobe a little, with my teeth.

'The perfect end to a negotiation,' she said.

'What?' I said.

She repeated what she said.

Starfish

When the man gets to thinking back on his life it seems to him that the secret of everything is contained in a few simple scenes. The scenes happen outside of him, perhaps inside some frame. For him the children are partly cold fact and partly his imagination. They are an amalgamation of every cheap encounter he ever had with them over the single year they lived with him. So far as children go, the girl and the boy were just fine. They went to school and returned home and ate incredible amounts of food and slept a little. Sometimes the man did not know where they were but they always surfaced in time for tea. The man worked and returned home and ate a little and slept whenever and wherever he could. When the man looks back on it, there is nothing which seems to distinguish that year from any other except that the children were present in it. Nevertheless, certain scenes endured.

The boy was maybe six, the girl a fair bit older, and they were throwing a ball between them on the lawn. The man was drinking a beer and watching them play.

'I haven't missed one yet,' the girl said. 'I've caught it every time.'

The girl threw the ball too hard at the boy. The boy missed.

'Don't throw it so hard,' the man said, taking a drink of his beer.

'That's not hard,' the girl said. 'I can throw it harder.'

The man encouraged the boy to take karate after school. The boy had no experience with sports and the man thought sports might do him some good. One night after karate the boy was standing in front of the television, showing the girl this move.

'This is how you do it,' he said.

His legs were spread wide and his fists were balled up in front of his face. He stood there before the girl, his belly poking out, jabbing his fists out one at a time but always returning them to his cracked, puffy lips. The girl made it clear his knuckles faced the wrong way.

'Your feet are too far apart,' she said. 'You're too open like that. Anyone could come in.'

She landed the boy a good one in the guts. The boy went down and lay there, stunned. But after a moment he recovered. He got to his feet and re-positioned himself, exactly as he had been.

'This is how you do it,' he said again.

He stepped closer to the girl, making the same useless jabs, backing her up against the coffee table that way. The girl had a look on her face which suggested she was deciding between one thing and the next but then she pushed passed him and went out.

Towards the end of that year the boy wanted to fish. He was sitting at the table next to the girl.

'You'll never catch anything,' the girl said. 'And anyway, if you do, he'll make you throw it back. Won't you, Dad?'

The man was reading the newspaper, which he lowered to answer the girl.

'If it was a baby,' he said. 'But he might catch something big.'

He raised and lowered his eyebrows until the boy laughed.

'He'll forget all about it in about five minutes flat,' the girl said. 'You watch.'

She pushed back her chair, left her dishes in the sink and went up the stairs. She had started wearing cut-off jean shorts and singlets with spaghetti straps. The music blasted all through the house when she turned it on.

The boy kept on at the man and the man took him out. On the river they didn't catch anything. The water moved beneath the tinny like the breath in the lungs of a dying man and the boy cried hard, all that fishing trip long. The man had a strong urge to smack him clean across the mouth. But when they got back to the car the boy suddenly stopped and the man had a big, pleasant feeling which became an idea.

'Let's trick her,' he said. 'Let's play a little joke.'

On the way home he pulled into the parking lot of a fish and chip shop. As they walked across the lot the boy slipped his hand into the man's. In the shop they stood together like that under fluorescent lights before the entire ocean turned inside out.

The boy wanted to play the trick on the girl. The man let him. The girl was crouched down by the pool, putting in the drops.

'Close your eyes,' the boy said.

He stood behind the black bars of the pool gate, grinning. The man was standing in the laundry doorway, drinking wine from a mug. The girl put the dropper in the box and shut the lid. She stood up.

'Close your eyes,' the boy said.

The girl closed her eyes.

The boy held up the fish.

'Look at this fish.'

The girl looked at the fish.

'Look at his whiskers,' the boy said. 'Look at this fish.'

The man winked at the girl, trying to tell her something, but the girl only stood there looking at the fish. The boy looked at the fish. It twisted on the line, its glassy gold eyes were fixed straight ahead.

That night they ate the fish. The man revealed the story of the fish. The girl didn't laugh or do anything to show she thought it was any good. After a while she said, 'This fish tastes like fish from the bottom of the sea. From the mud. This isn't normal fish. There's something wrong with it.' She pushed her plate away and looked at the man. 'There's something really wrong with it,' she said, like he hadn't heard her.

The man put down his fork. He was aware he was drunk so he kept his movements slow.

'Is there something I should do?' he said. 'You tell me what to do.'

The girl looked at him.

'You tell me what to do,' the man said. 'Because I don't have any idea, actually.'

The girl pushed her plate away. The boy picked his up and began to lick off the sauce. The girl looked at him, then back at the man.

'I'm not saying you need to do anything,' she said.

While the music blasted down the boy watched cartoons with the man. The man laughed first and the boy laughed, directly after.

Fishing went the way of everything else. Bike riding came next. The boy had trouble climbing the hills. The man rode close beside him, his hand on the boy's back. One time the girl went riding with them and when the ride was over she criticised the man.

'I never got pushed like that,' she said, 'when I was his age. Let him do it himself or he won't ever learn.'

'He's not like you,' the man said. He said it straight back. 'He never was like you, I imagine. And he never will be.'

That night the boy was too exhausted to eat and his limbs were so sore the man decided to rub him down with rosemary oil and then give him a salt bath. The phone rang in the middle of the bath.

'Father,' the girl said. 'It's Mother. Are you home?'

'Come up please,' he said.

The girl climbed the stairs.

'Can you watch him,' the man said, drying his hands.

He went down the stairs and picked up the phone. He listened as the woman he'd once loved more than he'd loved his own life told him of the direction of her life and of the role the children played in her life and of how much she loved them and how much she loved her life. Then she hung up. The man put the phone in the cradle and took the stairs two at a time but the girl didn't hear him coming back up.

She was sitting on the edge of the bath, considering the boy. He was laying the face washer flat and watching until it disappeared below the soapy water. When the girl spoke the boy looked up.

'We can do something,' the girl said. 'We can do something new. We can do something you've never done before. I think we should try.'

The girl leaned down into the bath and took a hold of the boy's ankles, pulling hard. His trunk and head slipped under the water and for a moment there was no sound. The girl looked through the water to her brother's peaceful face. She whispered:

'If, if, if, if.'

Then she let go of the boy's legs and he came screaming up.

He screamed like a horse with a bullet hole in his chest. The man went at the girl. He got her by the arm and pushed her up against the towel rack. The boy fell to soft whimpers and the girl began to laugh. The man let her go and stepped back against the wall. He lowered himself to the floor in an easy, liquid motion.

'I told you,' the girl said, taking a towel off the rack. She sat down again on the edge of the bath. 'Come here,' she said, reaching for the boy.

The boy leaned his head in. The girl began to towel it dry. The man watched all this with his knees drawn right up.

'I told you,' she said. 'Ten bucks she comes back.' She worked the towel around and into the boy's ears and his eyes were closed and his face was soft because he was enjoying himself. 'She'll be back before Christmas. She's never gonna last. Stand up.' She helped the boy climb out of the bath and wrapped the towel around him. 'Get your jarmies,' she said. 'I'll be in in a sec.'

The boy went off and the girl sat down beside the man. 'Don't worry,' she said. 'Something's happening to her we don't know anything about but she'll be back when it's over and then she'll take us back. See?'

The man looked at the girl. No, he didn't see. He put his arm around her and she lay her head against his chest and they sat together like this until the boy appeared shivering.

When the boy was in bed the man and the girl went downstairs. The man opened a beer and the girl ate some cheese. They sat in the living room with the television on and at some distant point they both fell asleep.

The next day was Saturday and the boy woke with the sun. The girl fried some eggs, which they ate in front of the television while the man rested on the couch, dozing on and off. When the girl's favourite song came on she put her plate on the coffee table and got up to dance. The boy watched her dance – her hips moved like sea water back and forth upon the sand. The boy got up to dance. Then he sat back down.

'You can dance,' the girl said. 'I'll show you how to dance.' She held the boy's hands and moved him around. 'This is how you do it.' She held his hands tight and she spun him around. 'You're dancing,' she said. 'Now do it yourself.'

She let go of his hands and lay down on the floor, flat on her back with her arms and legs spread wide out. Soon the boy copied her. And this is how the man thought he would always think of them – lying like two starfish on his living room floor.

The Gift

I wanted to say I was sorry, and to give you something. I think your loss is great. I think your loss might be the greatest loss there is, if I can put it like that. That young woman is dead and no words will bring her back. But there'll be flowers for her, won't there? There'll be such fine memories. And I wanted to give you a thing, if you'll just hear me out. A thing about your boy. It's just, I don't know what it is.

Now I don't know where exactly you lived in our town. Your boy got on at Battarack Lane. I know because I got on one stop before, at the square.

He was a beautiful kid to look at, for sure. Those dark curls. But his eyes were too blue, I always found that. He scared the hell out of me. I'm not ashamed to admit it.

When I heard what he did, I started telling my wife. She was sitting beside me in front of the television. He was bigger of course, he'd put on all that weight, but I would have known it was him anywhere. They were showing the pictures, the last ones of the girl. She walks past the bridal shop. That's it. She's gone. A moment after your son comes into view. Just seeing him again took me right back. I turned to my wife. Hannah, I said. I used to sit next to this kid on the bus. This most beautiful kid but my god, he was crazy.

He was crazy about dogs, I said. His mother bred dogs. These particular dogs, and he knew everything. We'd sit on the bus and he'd rattle it off, all about their bodies and their coats and their paws. They have a deep chest. They need extra space for their lungs. They have a long snout, for hunting. They hunt small animals and birds.

Okay, Hannah said. All right, that's enough.

Now my wife is a woman with a stomach, that's the thing, but even she couldn't listen to what I had to say in the end. She couldn't just sit there and have me go on. I had plenty more to say but in the end she got up and turned the television off. And I got her point. I really did. But let me just give you this one single thing. It's in the shape of a story but it only starts that way.

One day we were sitting on the bus and your boy turned to me. His eyes had grown dark. His skin was so pale, maybe that's what made his eyes look so dark. And he looked at me, I swear to god. He looked at me like he wanted something from me. And I said to him, what? What do you want? He said, I tried to put her back together. Those were his exact words.

I wanted to say something. I just couldn't think what. It was his eyes, how they'd changed, and the look on his face. Then he unzipped his schoolbag.

I'll tell you one thing – that smell is still in my head.

Now I don't know what your boy did to that dog. Maybe you know. Maybe it's nothing new. But I don't think the point is what he did to the dog. He was a boy, in that moment, who'd done something bad. And when he couldn't make it right he put it on his back. He carried it with him.

And now I'm giving it to you because I have to do it.

The Inhibitor

Karl sat in the driver's seat and turned the engine on. The man told him to do it, so he did. The man was old. He wore a high-visibility vest. Behind him his truck was parked. Its orange lights flashed.

'Try her now,' the man said.

Karl turned the key.

'Now,' the man said.

'No, nothing.'

The man knew everything under that hood. Pop the hood on an old car like that and underneath is this complete community of mansions and tunnels and heat and traps and a man like this knows every oiled neck in every one of those metal houses. How to scorn them, too, with the tips of his jagged fingers. Karl sat where he was and watched the man work. The sky was blue and the man's forearms were brown and the hood of the car was white. Earlier in the week, Karl had stripped a lot of the duco off the hood with the high-powered hose because he didn't have any idea how high-powered the hose would be. He couldn't notice it now. With the light of the sun through the sassafras tree, the hood appeared a perfect white and the brown of the man's forearms made it appear whiter still. An aeroplane went overhead and the man stepped out from under the hood.

'Try her now.'

Karl turned the key.

'Okay. Now.'

'No. Nothing.'

'All right, leave her there.'

'Take the key out?'

'Leave her there. Don't touch anything.'

Karl took his foot off the brake and his hand away from the key. On the street he stood close to the car but he didn't touch it. He looked under the hood where the man was doing things. Karl didn't have any clue what he was looking at and he understood just then that he never would. The man tapped a part.

'Alternator,' he said.

He tapped another part.

'Engine,' he said.

He did the same thing with the starting motor, tapping it with his finger and saying its name aloud. Karl thought he should take note, learn the names of the parts. It seemed to him that the bare minimum of what he needed to know in this world was being laid out for him but as soon as the words were said they were gone. The car choked and started.

'How'd you do that?' Karl said.

The man took a step back.

'Inhibitor,' the man said. 'Is there an alarm on this thing?'

'No,' Karl said.

'It's the inhibitor,' the man said. 'To stop someone stealing the car.'

'Somebody tried to steal my car?'

The man bent over the car again. He did something with his fingers and the engine cut.

'Nobody tried to steal this car. Try her now.'

Karl climbed into the driver's seat and pushed his foot hard onto the brake. He turned the key all the way.

'Turn the key.'

'I am.'

'Try her now.'

'No. Nothing.'

The man worked a little longer under the hood and Karl sat still at the wheel. He watched the tough skin of those forearms shifting in the light, now and then a flash of black fingers, a silver watch, triangles of the high-visibility vest, the soft grey of his hair. But mostly, Karl thought, the forearms.

'Yep,' the man said. 'You'll have to take her in. I'll get her started for you.'

'Okay. Thank you.'

That would be the life, Karl thought. Driving around in a truck with flashing lights, dropping in on people's lives and fixing things. The engine started. The man dropped the hood and came right up to the window.

'Tell them it's the inhibitor,' he said.

'Okay,' Karl said. 'Thank you.'

He put on his sunglasses. He put on his belt. The man had not moved.

'What will you say?' he said. 'When they ask what the problem is what will you say?'

'The inhibitor,' Karl said. 'There's something wrong with the inhibitor.'

'Good boy,' the man said. 'I'll get my truck out of the road.'

The man drove the truck down the road, turned right, and was gone. Karl followed the truck. The mechanic was that way. There wasn't any other way. But Karl was going the wrong way. He knew that as well as anything he'd ever known.

The Blue Dress

I had just moved into another room in another house and I had developed the habit of waking in the night to kneel on the floor and put both hands on my thighs and look directly in the mirror and marvel at my size. I would wake with a snap, the room would be dark but the light from the little blow heater would cast a weird blue glow and I would lie there wondering if the thing that had woken me would go away. I knew it was something specific, but I couldn't catch its name. Then it came to me through the blue dripping light – my size, my size, it was to do with my size. Something had grown and I did not know what it was. I got up, to sort it out. I thought by looking I might reveal something.

Sometimes in the mirror I was vaguely different shades of large but always I was so large it made my heart skip. The regular things went through my head to do with how I had gotten this way, but these never lasted because they were small things. The point was, there I was – a woman in the glass. Only my hands were a regular size.

Very occasionally, I would move my fingers in a pattern on my thighs, beginning with the pinkie and ending with the thumb. Watching this in the mirror gave me a creepy feeling and made me think of the fine silver of a spider's legs. I experimented with doing this and not looking directly at the hand. It took me some time to work the thing out but soon enough I came to realise that working in this way I could feel, quite distinctly, that the hand on my thigh belonged to someone else. This delivered a tremendous feeling in my spine and it was the reason I saved this particular experiment for special occasions. Most of the time, I kept my fingers still as I looked.

I looked and I looked. I looked for as long as I could. I softened my gaze so that my eyes were not popping so far out of my head and I was shocked, really shocked, at the way my eyes receded back inside my face so they became two slits, barely discernible. I fell into myself, lost in this way, then I got up and slid the glass aside. The dress was navy blue, printed with tiny flowers. The flowers were pink with shades of creamy white.

I had bought the dress for the wedding of a childhood friend. The day of her wedding was a good one for me. Her father had said, when he saw me, I never knew you could look so beautiful. I was wearing red lipstick and I felt happy with myself. Her father had looked at me and there was love in his eyes. This was a man I had known all my life but he'd never looked at me in the way he looked at me that day, at her wedding, in that dress. As I say I was wearing red lipstick as well but the look in his eyes was so deep and kind and I thought that's why my friend turned out so well because her father looked at her like this once or twice in her life. With those eyes.

I took the dress off the hanger and laid it out on the bed. Then I took off my tracksuit pants and my sloppy joe and I took off my t-shirt and I reached up my arms, I reached into the dress. Then, there I was, inside of it.

The zip of this particular dress was located at the side of the dress and it moved in the direction of the upper arm. I positioned my breasts on my chest strategically as I sucked in my breath and zipped up the dress. I returned my gaze to the mirror. I frowned at the sleeves which were a feature of the dress I did not exactly like, but it was true they finished in fine flutters of blue fabric slightly different to the rest. The dress hung off my body like it was made of water. And I remembered that night, I returned to myself, and I said to myself, it's all right, it's all right, it's all right, it's all right.

Happy Hour

David is visiting his mother at the psychiatric facility. She is permitted a visitor for one hour each week. David talks and talks. He has invented Vivienne, the girlfriend, but the rest of it is true. Later he will look back and understand the solution was absence, he should not have visited at all.

'This old crazy guy was yelling up a tree,' David says. 'Oh my god, Vivienne said, that poor man's lost his bird. He hasn't got a bird, I said, he's just some crazy guy. There aren't any birds around here.'

'Fancy that,' his mother says. She sits on the bed hunched over her crossed legs, hands folded in the centre of her lap. She has put on lipstick and there is a glob of red on her chin.

'We both stood there trying to work out what he was saying,' David says. 'He's calling for his bird, Vivienne said, I saw a sign before. There's no bird, Viv, I told her. He's just some crazy guy.'

His mother sits up and holds out her hand. For a moment David thinks the hand is extended for him but then he sees Eileen, leaning up against the door.

'Benign benign benign benign,' Eileen says. 'Benign benign benign.'

She enters, takes the hand, and buries it in her fleshy abdomen.

'Multiple benign lung nodules,' she says. 'I'm clear. Let's go.'

David looks at his mother, who gazes wetly up. He knows whatever is between these two has nothing to do with him.

'My son,' his mother says. 'He was saying. About a bird.'

'It's nothing,' David says. 'Anyway it's three o'clock.'

'Nothing!' Eileen says. She sits down on the bed.

He feels the back of his head growing hot, his bowels loosening. 'We said our goodbyes and the lights went for me to cross. I stopped. Vivienne said, you're going to go over aren't you? I said, yes. I went over to the man who was yelling up the tree. I said, have you lost your bird? He said, no. I said, do you have a bird? He said, no. I looked at the man and the man looked at me. I said, are you having a nice night? He said, yes.'

'Haha,' Eileen says. 'Hahahaha. That's nothing. When I was your age I came off my motorbike. It took them twenty-one hours to remove the gravel from my back. *De*-gloved. Four of them used tweezers but one used a soup spoon.'

His mother perks up.

'In the cupboard, David,' she says. 'I almost forgot.'

'Yes,' Eileen says. 'We made it in Craft.'

David opens the cupboard door, single, sanitary and white and stands in front of yet another freakish scarf.

'Eileen chose the colour.'

'Rainbow,' Eileen says.

'Do you like it, David?'

He looks down at her. Her face is so white, so soft, so composed. But the lipstick on her chin is a ridiculous joke.

'Mum. Can I do this? Let me just fix one thing.'

But his mother is leaning in towards the other woman's ear, saying something David can't hear and which he totally understands is not intended for him. He has the feeling he could kill. He could kill anything.

'We've got to go,' Eileen says. 'Your mother's concerned.'

'Next week?' his mother says.

'Of course,' David says.

His mother stands, unsteady. Eileen slips an arm around her waist and they disappear down the hall.

On the way to the train station David stops in front of a paperbark tree. He chooses a spot on the trunk and ties the scarf to it, pulling it tight. He decides on a spot where the mouth could easily be and punches this spot three times, each time harder than the last. Then he stands beside the tree and observes the blood on his knuckles. He is quite happy with the blood. For maybe an hour he is happy.

Voice of Dog

When the sun comes up and she stirs some and her boots get out the house you got to get your feet up your feet down turn around head down mouth closed nose up ears down feet wide apart and that's the most you got to keep your dog brains on doing. But half the guys here can't keep their brains on doing it. They got to yell out or they got to be too damn calm and they got to bang hard on the bars just to stop from falling all the way but they get rapped and they yell some and none of us got nothing to say to that at all. Today it's minutes long and the rain comes down. The trees outside sway and the leaves hang long and limp and it takes a while to recall they're not trees at all at least none such trees as I recall there was trees at home. And I'm thinking those trees are being there and all when just what's there is grey wall. That and the bricks thick as mud and the sky that don't get talked to that often anymore.

Yeah the rain comes down and I can hear the storm a way off. What else I can hear is folk music along with the rain and all of a sudden the wet smell of the air comes along the strands of newness pouring down and the trees out there are so tall and thin and the leaves aren't falling too much and the cars pass one by one by one by one along the road over there way out past the fence and the rain coming is getting louder and in the background are the drums and the saxophone and the electric guitar and further off in the distance a sort of laughter. That's it every afternoon here. Just outside my room.

She'll feed us soon. She will or one of them will. We'll stand at the window each one of us alike each one of us made of steel confixed of multiple squares we'll stand there like hurricanes but we'll be so still you can't tell. In this place there is only steel for looking through. Concrete to rest the head. In this place there are guys that get you just with a look and you know nobody in here not one of these guys in here nobody that was ever a child is in here some of these guys.

I leave off the window. I take a drink of rainwater and it settles me. I look at the concrete wall and think of getting my brain into it and taking charge of the cold concrete so you can't tell no difference between one and the next. And the sound of a train I've never heard before is whooshing. Such a high-pitched such an urgent sound and I'm feeling so fucken antsy I hope that motorbike man don't look at the sign at the crossing at the lights. I'm so zapped here I hope to hell the killer scream of his engine goes dead right on the track between metal and metal. But even if it did those trains would keep coming. I just want quiet but those trains just keep coming. Jesus those trains. If it isn't the wet dog smell or the motorbike it's a fucken train. I take another drink and take it up easy too. It helps. I need to work this out. It won't do no good if I don't work this out.

My flank through that river was marching and wet. Wet mud up the bank my ribs chorused and my muscles twitched as she pulled me deeper under and my body moved out. Under there I swear was a transient liquid world. Green and quiet. But when I made it to the bank I looked back and it was black. A frozen black with her yellow hair resting on the surface like a glove and me with the mangroves feeding up between my paws. These stupid fucken things with which no bastard can hold on. Hold on. I'm keening now. I'm thinking once things were different and could be again.

This place becomes more like a greenery through the bars. Intermittent. A nursery with leaves rained on with tinsel and the flowers have mirrored leaves that don't leave me alone. I am staring at them as if they are planted into the concrete outside the shed where the boys sometimes sit around a burning smoking pit. They smoke and they talk digging their boots in the rolling flames but the heels don't go so far since it's only gravel in this place. Gravel laid across the thin crumblesome earth shallow as a layer of her fixed magenta cunt. I am well prepared for combat I think this to myself. It will be relentless and four hundred people might die. I think why's it up to me to break them down? I'm after the rats.

I breathe and drop my tongue but the rainwater is gone. The greenery dispenses and I close my eyes and set down my head and I listen to the storm coming along the highway from the river. The itch spreads inside out as the river does along the road. The fact is you live your whole life and it's not worth a cent. It sure is something to recall it the way things used to be when your whole life was taking place and you didn't think a thing. It sure is something but it doesn't stop the burn. I can't get to scratch it the hairline of the earth. It is incumbent.

You see I began with language some thousand days ago. It is a mystery. I close my eyes with my whole face and hold my limbs as tight as I can and a fire shoots through my skin and lights up my bones. I must register the itch and not attend to it I know. The blood comes too easy and the boys have a way. They'll appear for no reason in the middle of the day with the horns all a-glowing from the knobs in their backs and their pinnacle eyes. You want to avoid it and look good for sale.

Some guy across the way is crying up now. Crying up so bad he starts up a circus. Well you better shut up I tell him but some guys you can't say nothing to without them getting all sparky and mean. Shut up if you want a feed I tell the guys and they do. I tell them she'll feed us soon but there's no sign from the house and I know that and they do. And so they cry. Some guys they'll cry no matter what you say. And if you don't say a thing they'll cry all the same until the sun gets away and the night comes across. They'd go mad then some of those guys for how deep the night is and how long it stays until their bodies and minds are all so fed up with their grassing and crying all day they got to sleep. A lot of the time they can't do nothing but sleep. The smell of wet dog keeps coming in and I sure am scared of the motorbike coming back and screaming through my head and through my heart and I hope to hell he dies in the instant. Such a hide any guy who kills the quiet like that.

The rain comes down and spits in through the bars. The floor is black with puddles so if you dive in headfirst you might find some place where your head doesn't hurt anymore so you swim. It never hurt to go down to the river with my girl. You had to be careful about the bees but that was naturally it. They never troubled. She never strayed far from me once we'd passed the post. I showed her a rat skinned clean by bull ants and hidden deep inside the foliage and she considered it this big catastrophe and I chased her with it consoling her but then she cried. I dropped the rat. It was nothing to me. Not then. Though what I'd do for a carcass of a thing now for any old thing to say that it was there and mine I cannot say. Words fail me and were not made for this. This. In a cold concrete room. I cannot understand how I did not smell the thing. The thing that would alter her I have no memory of it. I never saw it coming and I've never seen it since. I missed something vital and I do not know what it is.

Well I leave off that time because I have to. Through there isn't anything but rain here again and gone again and the dead empty house and no river and no trees. No mud. Just this concrete space concrete world and guys crying out for a thing that's not there. One boy on a bike won't make a scrap of difference to those tracks spilt all over them and I just want quiet now my god but those trains. Just keep coming. Jesus those trains. If it isn't the wet dog smell or the sound of the fucken bike it's a goddam train. And I can't hardly believe what the truth of it used to be.

She'll feed us soon. But it doesn't do no good to stand here and talk about it. That's what kills them some of these guys. They stand there in their big rooms near the big house and they talk. They talk this way when the new kids come in all skinny and split fur burnt raw with cigarettes and the fleas on them as big as roaches. I study the wall. It is hopping with fleas. I say one or two things to them but those bastards lay low. The rain pulls off a bit I need to go but there isn't anywhere in here to go but against the fucken wall.

Nothing for this pull but a cold-pressed solid walk. I pace. Up and down back and forth I can't go there so I'll itch. That's one thing to feel. One thing at a time. I back up against the wall and rub until it hurts. I have to go now but there is no way. The rain rushes down now. The storm starts to spread I lie down to be good in it but it doesn't do no good that's why I'm telling you this.

I really have to get out. This much is clear. Some way I'll have to get out from here or I'll go completely mad. Perhaps I can get back across inside the rain. Across the faking sunshine and out onto the road. Through the bush after that and some way off in the distance my home. Maybe there's still some way I can go back. Because she was my girl but I never recognised her.

She was full of water on the bank. I chastised her I raged I was incredibly rude. A neighbour showed up. A bastard with a beard and something to wrap her in. They wanted to keep me but wanting doesn't matter. They couldn't do. I couldn't do. She was mine she was mine I was hers she was mine. But there were too many flowers. There were flowers everywhere. I was drunk on purple flowers and I couldn't smell a fucken thing.

She'll feed us soon. I lie down close my eyes. There are footsteps in my head but it's all black in front of me. The smell the shame the fury and some guy's having a laugh let him go let him go. I suppose that's her coming now to feed us. Then we'll go then we'll go. The windows will burst up and the sky will pour in and the bars will be gone and the rain will fall steady. As we run.

It's very strange how the pictures come. They come they go they come they go and they are breaking on in when all I want is a feed. All the while the train is going on its track and you can't keep a track of it. I look again out the window and the dark has come down. I push my nose into the space between the window and the floor. Try to catch the breeze. My teeth grind. She'll feed us soon. Lord knows that she will. Lord knows it's work work work to stay still in this place. Still still still still. Fifty-nine million years I tell you and I never heard no fucken train.

Love is a Human Emotion

I think I'm in love with my fertility specialist. I haven't met her yet. But I've seen her photograph on her website, and the photographs of her happy family and their ragdoll and their swimming pool. I've read her description of everything she'll do to me, and her description of all the mechanics of what my body will do to itself, in return. I've waited my whole life, it seems, for somebody to know what they're doing with me. For somebody to love me in a productive way, a way which leads to somewhere, which ends in something. An ending that is also a beginning.

I know I'm in love because this is the same way I've felt about a lot of other women, going back. This is a primary love, an archaic love. It is so deep and dark, so tangled and twisted, so speckled with red roses, so lit up with silver horses and sugar roof-tops, it's practically a myth.

But look at the sweet lines, curving down from her lips. Look at her eyes, so clear and bright, staring right down the barrel of the camera. You can tell she knows what she's doing – that you turn up on her doorstep with your fertility concerns and she snaps on her gloves, turns on her tube. There is a glint in her eye because she knows what to do and this knowledge is scientific but it is also true to her. This is not desperate or useless knowledge. It is of women for women. Whereas the man comes past tense, frozen, in a jar. The kind of plastic jar you piss into.

I think I'm in love with my fertility specialist. It's everywhere this love, but mostly it's in the skin. In the blood, the bones – there is no test for this. Nothing you can excrete, no swab you can take to measure the presence of this rotten disease. Help, I'm in love with a healthcare professional, again!

'Oh, it's a pattern,' I said to myself out loud, down at the bay on a night after a full day of rain so the bay had swelled up to twice its ordinary volume.

'Look how full and soft the water is, my girl.' I said this to my dog, who was trotting behind me. We passed several people but it was dark and I was fine to continue talking in this way.

'This is the way I'll reassure my baby, when it comes,' I said. 'Anyway, isn't this the form and function of the nursery rhyme?'

Nobody answered me. The boats bobbed on the full, dark water. The cars, one by one, rolled over the bridge.

Perhaps this love is simply evolutionary? The drive to merge reproduction with human bonding and personal/financial safety? A fertility specialist would be just right for me. She'd be out of the house all day making people's dreams come true and I could just sit at home and count the babies.

This love has never been an appropriate force. Once upon a time I loved my mother like this. I loved my sister this way, which did not go so well. You can't marry your own sister! I grieved over this. It also struck me as devastating that I could not marry my own father for he had – long ago – already taken a wife. I was caught in this incredible web. I went in for the love but I did not come out. I looked everywhere!

As time went by, this became a specific catastrophe because I never stopped, regarding the love. Apart from immediate family members, who I no longer lust over, and one particular teacher who I still see about the place, whose hair has thinned, and who is now not even remotely interesting to me, whoever I have loved I continue to love and I continue to lose since whoever I love does not love me back.

When I was a child, and woke in the night, I would lie outside my parent's room, my face pressed up to the dark horizontal space between the door and the floor. I was breathing the air they were breathing in there. I knew it was not appropriate to knock on the door, to enter the room, but I was frightened – so frightened – so I stayed still down there. Sometimes a big black cockroach went by, all shiny and supremely confident, and that's why I'm not at all afraid of cockroaches. I would lie there and lie there and breathe in the black air. I could breathe in what they were breathing but I could not get in.

That was the dilemma. Now, what's the problem?

I think I'm in love with my fertility specialist. I haven't met her yet. I plan to make an appointment to start off this love, to discuss my specific fertility situation with this qualified specialist. I've been thinking the love I have could be thrown all the one way. You know, towards a child. Perhaps my life is over and a real, healthy love will never happen for me, but perhaps what I could do is I could make something of this love? Another human being, for example? A member of this species? Who, with a little luck, might have a much better time of it on this particular planet than me? Who, with a bit of luck and some good-enough parenting strategies, might know what to do with their love?

Love is a human emotion. Dogs do not have it. Emus, rats, fish. Only humans have to manage their love, or die trying.

'I do not want to die!' I said to the bay. 'Without even knowing what real love is!' It was a curious audience. The water slapped the concrete wall and the boats went tinkle tinkle.

I think I am in love with my fertility specialist. I do not love the font on her website – Palatino Linotype, magenta, 12 – but I love all the things she says she will do for me.

My role is to care for you and your future child, she says. *I'll keep a close eye on your ovaries to determine when your eggs are mature. At the right time you'll inject the medication yourself.*

I think of all the medication I have given to myself over the years.

Listening to instructions is crucial, she says. *Practice deep breathing before penetrating the skin. Numb the injection site with ice. Inject with someone you love. Plan a reward so you feel less dread.*

This is the paragraph which sells her to me.

For most women the egg collection is considered 'the big day'. I will insert a needle into each ovary. Using this technique I will drain your follicles.

In my mind my eggs are jumping up and down, each of them dressed in a hot pink parker. 'It's been so long!' they chorus. 'Let us out!' they chime. 'It's been thirty-seven years, sister! Drain! Drain! Drain! Drain!'

Your eggs will then be distributed to a scientist, who will closely observe them under a microscope. You are welcome to observe this process taking place.

Come Henry, come Audre, come Luna, come George! Come out! Come out, children! Come out, come out, come out!

The strongest embryo will be targeted and placed into your uterus. An additional hormone is given to keep the uterus quiet, giving the embryo the optimal chance to implant.

Well I'll need extra hormones, this occurs to me. My uterus shouts and hollers, my uterus bellows. How am I meant to make this decision, it says. How am I meant to make this decision – and alone!

I think I'm in love with my fertility specialist. I haven't met her yet. She ends her speech with a signature, a contact email, and a number to call. Her face is to the left of her explanation. It looks so kind and gentle. Her hair is so straight. I think of what lengths I have gone to for love. Unsuitable, imagined love. Now, give me that phone.

Mammals

No matter what Tessa did she could not get the child to say 'panda'. The child was absolutely fine with other animals. She could name 'camel' and 'elephant' and 'monkey', obviously. She couldn't yet differentiate between 'lion' and 'tiger' but she was coming along with 'hippopotamus', pronunciation-wise, and she wasn't even two years old. Tessa thought the child was probably advanced because when she finished the *Mammals* book she always took her time with the back cover where, down the bottom near the barcode, there were four small images of the other books in the series: *Reptiles, Amphibians, Molluscs* and *Fish*. Each of the titles had a different coloured cover and following a close inspection of these images the child always posed the same question: Where's green? Tessa had to explain how *Mammals*, with its bright green cover, did not feature on the back cover of the book because the book was itself.

The child chose not to take this response to heart. Tessa knew this because she posed the same question every time. Other things – such as how to work the adhesive tabs on a new nappy for Dolly – the child only had to be shown the one time and ever after performed the task upon request with diligence. This was part of the reason Tessa was growing suspicious. She decided to raise the situation with the child, matter-of-fact. The child had cost her a good deal of time and money and she did not appreciate this latest ruse. There had been other ruses. Once, during the meeting with the father, the child had proclaimed 'Da-da', out of nowhere. The child had not said a single word until then. The child's name meant elegant tinkling of jade in Mandarin but Tessa was lately feeling that she didn't deserve it.

Tessa decided to raise the issue with the child over breakfast. She sat the child in the highchair before a plate of bread thick with jam. Behind her, out the window, the buildings of the city were all quiet, dark glass but soon the sun would pierce through them and light up the room. Tessa pulled up a chair. She lay the book across her lap.

'I don't know what you are getting at,' she said, 'what you are trying to achieve with the whole panda thing. I can tell you right now I won't stand for it.'

She paused, to give the child a chance to digest.

'You are two next month and then you will be three. After that four, five, six, etcetera. You will become increasingly cognisant. Right now you don't know anything much but you know some things and you'll not keep them from me. I am your mother. There are options.'

There was no way of really knowing if the child understood. Certainly she paid attention. She was decorous in this sense. She chewed carefully, smacking her lips around and feeling everything with her tongue. She finished what was in her mouth before she took anything new. She was in no rush. Tessa picked up the book and opened it. She positioned the book so the child could see. She pointed to the picture of the animal, making a friendly puhp-puhp sound with her finger on the page.

'Camel,' the child said.

'Good girl,' Tessa said.

She turned the page.

'Elephant,' the child said.

'Good girl. Well done.'

Then Tessa shut the book.

'Now the panda is easy,' she said. 'Perhaps the easiest of all. Everyone knows what a panda bear is. The panda is iconic, a conservation reliant species. Its diet is ninety-nine per cent bamboo. Molecular studies reveal the panda is a true bear, part of the family Ursidae, even though the precise taxonomic classification has been debated for some time. Nineteen million years ago it differentiated from the main ursine stock. Nineteen million years in the making.'

She opened the book to the panda page and held it up for the child to see.

'The thing to know,' she said, 'is that there is an almost identical bear, called the Qinling bear, which I do not expect you to handle vernacularly but which is worth knowing about purely because it has been excluded from popular forms of literature such as your book. Now the Qinling bear is exactly the same as this bear but he has bigger molars and his patches are more often brown on brown. The white in the panda bear is the dominant colour, but he has distinctive black patches around the eyes, ears, muzzle and across the middle of his body. This is all evident in the picture you are seeing. Are you paying attention?'

The child turned her head, slowly, from side to side. Her mouth was partially open and there was jam on her cheek which glowed like a wound.

'The thing with Qinling bear,' Tessa said, 'is there is no way of knowing which brown is correct. On the second-last day of August in the year I was born, something happened. A female Qinling panda, called Dan-Dan, was brought to the Xi'an Zoo to mate with a regular panda bear. The mating was successful. The offspring were born black and white but within a few days their colours turned to brown and then the three babies died. There are no pictures of them on the internet and they have not been turned into soft toys.'

The child opened and closed her mouth as if there were food inside. She did not react when it was clear there was nothing. Merely, she repeated the action.

'Panda,' Tessa said, making the puhp-puhp on the page. 'Can you say panda? Panda bear.'

But the child was stuck on the image of the bear — the bright white fur and the sudden onset of black. Tessa was stuck, too. Ninety-nine per cent bamboo, she thought. And: nineteen million years! How is it possible, Tessa thought, that in nineteen million years not one single hair has ever strayed? This confirmed for her in the instant the weight of the recurrence of the infinitesimal life. She faltered.

'Well what is it?' she said. 'You say what this is.'

But the child was transfixed. Her brown eyes grew wet and her bottom lip dropped. Her eyelids fluttered. Tessa leaned forward, breathing hard.

'Wake up!' she shouted. 'Do not go to sleep!'

A hot line of sun shot through the window. The child blinked several times, in rapid succession.

'Dan-Dan,' she said. 'Dan-Dan.'

Tessa sat bolt upright. The child began to cry, a serious sudden sound, but Tessa was taken with the way the light moved — the way the yellow strands of sunlight played across the walls and the floor in unforeseeable patterns, moving constantly in their flickering decree but having no effect. The light had arrived but it hadn't changed anything.

Sitting there, the child victorious again, Tessa felt the full force of her human grief that the vision before her did not have a name.

Turtle

It's strange to be so old and thinking of rape. I don't believe I thought of rape much as a boy, and if I did I didn't know it. I allow myself to think freely on it now, how I'd like to rape her, there is nothing to stop me and only me here to fancy how loving her that way would be such a pleasant thing. She is not my daughter. And there are things to think far worse than this. Where I've been and what I've seen, yeah, there are worse things than thinking how I'd like to jam my pent-up, rock-hard balls in her mouth. How I'd like to do it with her eyes closed and her pretending to be asleep. I know it's not appropriate or acceptable to admit but every morning now the light comes and I don't know what it is that's got me thinking this way. I've done all the right things in my life, so it were. I used to spy on my wife but apart from that I haven't done anything.

The girl I'd like to rape lives in the apartment opposite me. She is big and strong, always going somewhere. She wears short skirts and thick black tights. I say, are you off? She laughs. I laugh. She is a spectacle in her tights. Christ those thighs. I am just an old man with a bucket watering the kangaroo paws, my hair thin and white, my legs wasted, holding my bucket with both hands and doing my job. I roll out the bins one by one every Tuesday afternoon and the building manager ignores the grass I smoke at night. I blow the smoke out my kitchen window which faces the carpark. Once, while smoking, I saw a turtle. A big turtle she was, as big as any car out there. The turtle reared up on her back legs and waved her front feet at me. Then she crawled away at her implausible pace. I look for her occasionally, out my window at night. And when I don't see her I look for anything at all. Sometimes cars come in and out but apart from that nothing happens on this street.

I used to spy on my wife in the morning. The baby was brand new and we were already sick of him. He wanted feeding constantly. All he wanted was feeding, holding. He always wanted singing to. I was working day and night.

I would return home and fall into bed. I'd reach for my wife when I wanted her but she had nothing for me. I thought of a carcass. I thought of a fish. She was up and down endlessly to the baby's constant cries. Sometimes she'd be so tired, so sore, she wouldn't even bother to put her dressing gown on. The two of them, her naked, locked like that next to me. I was trying to sleep. I made it clear to her. I said, that makes me sick. It really did make me sick to see her feeding the baby this way, him guzzling, her breasts so big, her nipples prehistoric in their size, when did they turn *purple*? I hadn't signed up for this. But when I woke to her absence in the bed the silence in the bedroom grated on me. I went after her, quietly.

She was in the sunroom, facing the window. Just a little light was coming through under the curtains. Her back was so pale, so white and so broad, the gentle mounds of her vertebrae were showing through, she had her knees wide apart and a pillow on her legs for the baby. I saw, from behind, how now and then her head dropped down, then jerked back up. I had a terrible wanting. I wanted to get down on my knees behind her and kiss the top of her spine. But I could smell her and I could smell the milk and the awful baby smell. I was young and I didn't know how to love. I didn't know it had a smell and a consistency. I went back to bed and dreamed of so much nothing.

I know what kind of turtle she is, now. I looked her up. The size and weird style of her has all been explained to me. She's a leatherback sea turtle, the heaviest modern reptile that's not a crocodile. I like to think of her as modern. That is some comfort to me. I smoke my rotten grass and I think of her size but mostly what I think of as I smoke is her shell. Her shell is not a shell, for instance – it's a build-up, a covering of skin and oily flesh.

I finish my joint. I grind it out in the sink. I stand there, holding onto the sink, looking out the kitchen window. I come to a surprising realisation.

Say I had a choice. Between the turtle and the girl. Say someone comes along and I am offered a choice. What will it be? he says, holding out one hand. On the one hand, he says, you get to rape her. Rape her as hard and as long and as brutal as you like. Afterwards she'll forget. She'll recall none of it. There won't be a single bruise upon her pretty neck. On the other hand, he says, the turtle returns. The turtle? I say. (How could he know this?) The turtle, he says, returns.

I wait for him to go on. I know what I would choose. But suddenly I'm distraught. I hold hard to the sink. My god, I cry out. My god, where is she? And: how could her back be made of skin and oily *flesh*. Isn't she a turtle! My god, where is her shell!

I start to cry. Out of love for this creature I have seen once in my life. This magnificent creature, in the most unlikely place.

Autumn

Ada was going to kill herself. She had just bought some nice, new rope. It was blue. This had struck her as so unlikely in the shop.

'Do you have any other rope?' she had said to the boy.

'Like longer rope?' he said. 'Or do you mean thicker rope?'

'I'm not sure,' Ada said.

'Well, what do you want it for?'

'Oh, it's fine,' Ada said. 'I guess this will do.'

She walked home through the city. The air was crisp. It was newly autumn, which everyone knows is the saddest time of year. Ada was not sad. The sky was blue and there were several clouds. There were orange flowers growing out of a wall. Everything was fine. The rope was in her bag. The clouds, the flowers in their place. Even the trees stuck in the pavement were fine, Ada thought. It had been fifty-two years. She would not make it fifty-three. This she could do. Nothing had changed. The air was cool in her nostrils. She also felt it in her ears. She was moving with great purpose. She felt happy and free.

In her apartment building Ada took the lift up. When the doors opened she turned right in the direction of her place but she paused on account of a movement underneath the window.

The dog was of medium size. He was the shade of a jersey caramel and he was standing still, under the window. The cleaner came down the hall pushing her trolley along. She stopped in front of Ada.

'Good morning, Ada,' she said.

'Morning,' Ada said.

The dog stayed where he was but now his tail was going side to side.

'Your dog, mam?' the cleaner said.

'Dogs aren't allowed,' Ada said. 'I suppose we should call security.'

The phone was pinned to the wall opposite the lifts. For a moment both women stood there looking.

While the cleaner made the call, Ada watched the dog. He moved around the foyer in a frank, easy way. This irritated Ada. He was strong, broad across the shoulders, and he didn't seem concerned he was interrupting anything. He paused and put his nose to things and went on lapping the foyer. Ada called once to the dog and the dog came along.

'Sit,' Ada said.

The dog sat. The cleaner returned.

'They're calling council,' she said. 'They'll meet you downstairs.'

'Okay,' Ada said.

'How will you hold on to him?'

Ada reached into the bag. She brought out the rope and tore off the cardboard packaging.

'I can take that,' the cleaner said. She held out her hand.

'Thank you.' Ada made a noose in three swift motions and slipped it over the dog's head. She tightened it slightly. 'Is that right?' she said.

'Looks good,' the cleaner said. 'Will you be okay?'

They both looked at the dog. He looked up at them.

'I'll be fine,' Ada said. 'Thanks for your help.'

Ada took the fire stairs down. The dog moved lightly, a touch in front, but then he pulled away and Ada lost her grip on the rope. At the bottom of the stairs was a print with shattered glass. The print showed a child, sitting in a bath, looking into a mirror from which a pink rat looked back. The dog lifted his leg and pissed on the rat. Ada picked up the rope and pushed open the door.

The ranger arrived in a white van with the council logo on the side. He handed Ada the paperwork and swiped a scanner over the dog.

'No microchip, mam.'

Ada filled out the form and handed it back. The ranger opened the back of the van and let a ramp down. Ada stepped back.

'Oh, I don't know,' she said. 'I don't know about a cage.'

'It's a crate,' the ranger said.

Ada looked at the cage.

'What if I take him myself?'

The ranger shook his head.

'It's in the system now. We have to put this through.'

'Just for a walk,' Ada said. 'The owner might show up.'

'You called us in,' the ranger said. 'We have to put it through.'

It took both Ada and the ranger, pushing hard above the tail, to get the dog up the ramp, in the van.

'Oh, wait,' Ada said. 'That's my rope. It's new.'

The man reached into the cage. He slipped the rope off the dog and gave it to her.

'Have a nice day,' the ranger said.

'Thank you. You too.'

Ada returned to her apartment. She looked at the rafters. She looked at the chair. She was awfully tired. She thought she might lie down. Just for a little minute. She lay down on the floorboards in the hallway. The boards were cold on her skin. She closed her eyes. She thought of orange flowers. She thought of white snow. As she started to drift off she decided she'd go after the dog. She would phone up the council, fill out more forms, bring him home.

She was asleep when the banging started on the door. She opened her eyes and listened.

Tolerance

When she's strung out she smells the same in the morning but she says crazy things like my brain is on fire. I feel like road kill, she says. It's just the absence I can't fill.

I am so distressed to hear her say such things but I tolerate it and kiss her on the cheek, on the neck. This is a cheek, this a neck, I have learned how to love. I have learned this love with assistance from her. She is my wife. I am married to her.

My wife, it's true, can go one way or the next. She can say, you need to leave. I'm feeling violent – you should go. She can say, I'm breaking down. I'm about to ruin this relationship. She says such things often. She is incredibly articulate. I fell in love with her some time ago and I haven't come out. I'm not looking to come out and I never will. This is love.

It's still love when I am on the street with all my bags packed. I get as far as the pub. There are people over there with their trackies down around their ankles placing bets. Nobody pays attention! A sick man and a sick dog cross the street against the lights. I get to these lights and I can't go on anymore.

She texts me first. She says, I'd never leave you on Christmas Day. She uses my full name in the text so I know it's my fault. You asked me to leave, I text back. I'm respecting your choice. I haven't left, I say, yet. Anyway.

This is a fairly new marriage and I have not yet worked out all the rules. I thought that the relationship would go one way or the next. Black or white thinking. Yes, this is me. And I actually think of my father so much, these days, from this position I am in with these very cold feet. So cold. I think of my father with my mother's head on his lap and me at the kitchen bench, chopping carrots.

My wife has simple passions. She works fast but her natural state is to take things very slow. She used to say to me, to my face, I'm completely in love with you. She used to say, you are the hottest thing. The hottest thing I have ever seen. Sometimes she would tell me I had a problem with my emotions and I would have to go ahead and hide my face from the shame. It's okay, she would say. Don't be ashamed.

The signs were there but I was committed to her because I loved her and this was my life.

The Hoarder's House

It was one of those Sundays when the girlfriend was away and I was scared because I felt right on the edge of something I'd been on the edge of for some time.

'Eli,' I said, pushing open his door. 'Mate.' He was lying curled into himself on the bed in his hoody and his footy shorts. 'Come on.'

He swore and shook his head and pressed his hands either side of his head so his curls showed like shadows between his wide, brown fingers.

'They've lost it,' he said. 'I can't believe it.'

He gave this deep, stupid moan and then started to cry because when it came to football he didn't hide how he cried and that was something I deeply despised about him. At the same time, I was desperate to get down on the bed. What I wanted to do was position myself around the whole back of his huge body, put my arms around his arms and hold him like he were a stone.

'What about the hoarder's house?' I said. It was the right thing to say because he army rolled off the bed. 'You'll love it. There's a car parked in the drive, buried up to the roof.'

As he pulled his shoes on I got a long look at his legs. They were the deepest, strongest legs I think I have ever seen with this incredible spread of white thigh at the top which I wanted to bear down on, for some reason, with my knee.

The pavement was still wet from the rain and our shoes made a sticking sound as we walked. I had a feeling in my mouth like I might take some big step I'd been meaning to take after which point I'd never be myself again. Or I'd be myself but I just wouldn't be the same.

'I don't get it,' Eli said.

'It was a soft try,' I said.

We followed the train line and walked over the bridge past the school where there was a tree full of black cockatoos. I wanted to show them to Eli, to see if he would react any particular way, but when we got to the tree it was empty of birds. Perhaps on account of the rain.

'Come on,' I said, 'it's somewhere up here.'

Eli tied up his hair in a perfect little bun and I tried really hard not to zoom in on his head, the part of his skull showing through underneath the shave, which he'd only got done because the girlfriend requested it. I'd lie in my room and think on his head. His hot head resting in the cave of my abdomen. My hands on his head. On the back of his neck.

'They've lost their way,' Eli said. 'That's the season right there.'

'They're finished,' I said. 'Hang, on. Let me get this right.'

At the intersection I stopped. I decided on right though I was thinking of left and we crossed over the bridge which was mainly blocked off. I went in front of Eli and he followed me along. When I saw the brick wall at the front of the hoarder's house, I slowed down. It was the time of day just before everything turns its proper shade of dark. I opened my eyes wide, trying to see everything, but the sky was violet ink and the trees were so dark and the air was so cold in my eyes I felt blind.

'It's just up here,' I said.

I had the terrible feeling it might be too dark to see. I thought perhaps I had made a grave error bringing Eli to the hoarder's house at this time of day, when the lack of light would affect the experience, disturb the full impact of the scene. Then it occurred to me the hoarder might be home and sure enough, as we came to it, I saw the porch lights were on.

'Christ Almighty,' Eli said.

I showed him what I thought were the divisions in the yard.

'See it's arranged into squares,' I said. 'I think it's ordered somehow.'

Eli jumped up on the brick wall, his arms in the air. The brick wall was low and he performed this act in a single motion.

'Hey, mate,' I said. 'Eli.'

But he had already jumped off with a theatrical leap, and I thought of those coloured ball pits I had loved as a kid. He shouted and scrambled to his feet, sending crap everywhere. He held up a black frame, the middle of a bike, then he threw that down and picked up the next thing.

'Eli,' I said. 'Come on, buddy.'

But he was kicking and falling and crawling through the junk, making his way towards the car in the drive. I looked up at the hoarder's house, expecting something to occur. The porch was all quiet.

'I'm going,' I said. 'I'm going. Let's go.' I stood there and watched as he climbed up, onto the bonnet of the car. 'Hey. Mate.' That's all I said.

Then I walked off, with the sound of him hooting cutting through the cold air as the night settled in and the objects took their shape.

When I got home I made myself a drink and finished it off pretty quick. Then I made myself another, larger drink and sat down in front of the television. I began to feel better as the heat of the whiskey went straight to my head and I decided I would be fine, the whole stupid thing could end there. Perhaps I'd move out, maybe I'd move to the beach, and just before I left I could tell it to him straight in the only words I had. Or I could tell it to him tonight. Perhaps he'd say something back. I decided this was it, I was ready, I was drunk and I felt like myself and I would tell him I was completely in love with him, just like that. But then I heard him coming home, dragging something heavy down the drive. I turned off the television in a hurry and took my drink into my room.

Franklin Street

Molly once spent some time in a psychiatric hospital. It was pretty rough. The hospital was located on Franklin Street. All along Franklin Street on both sides of the street the flame trees grew. They were naked at the tip, stripped and raw and grey, but the leaves were thick and full around the middle of the trunks and the leaves, when they fell, coloured the grey cold of the pavement a wonderful gold.

Every morning at the hospital Molly attended group. It involved a semi-circle of plastic chairs positioned before a nurse who was herself positioned in front of a shining whiteboard. There were no pens. The chairs were the kind girls sit in at school. The problem was it reminded them of school.

They were all girls at the hospital. They were all ugly. It was unbelievable how ugly they were. One of them might have been pretty, but she'd done something to her hair that revealed her eggy forehead and her sort of squinty eyes, which weren't a feature in the least. That girl was of little interest to Molly. None of them were of any interest to her in a good way but two of them tormented her.

One was called Florence, she was maybe twenty years old. She had deep craters on her chin and her cheeks and she had this problem with stealing her grandmother's medication and taking it herself. She'd been busted. The other one had a name Molly could never recall, something like Suzanne. Suzanne was the ugliest of them, not including Molly, on account of some condition she had going with her face. It was very much like someone had sliced off her lips and she'd applied a lot of lipstick to what was left. Thinking this way gave Molly the terrible turn. It was a turn in her abdomen, where she was feeding again, a raw red turn the shape of the earth that gave her the feeling her heart had dropped down several floors. But Molly should not say a thing about Florence or Suzanne. They were sitting where they were meant to sit in that room on their chairs, while Molly writhed on the floor, banging her head against the salmon pink wall. Every bang she made came up against a terrible pause and in the pause she heard the traffic rolling by on Franklin Street. The sound of the yellow leaves falling off the flame trees were echoes in her head and she had a very strong sense of the minutiae of things, the pores in her face and the veins in the weeds which grew up through the cracks of the brick wall outside the hospital. This kind of thinking was a troubling sign but it came down on her like this some days and she beat her head on the wall beside the empty fireplace, keeping time.

'Molly,' the nurse said. 'Come take a seat. Let's check in.'

The nurse was called Prue. Prue was very sweet. She wore snazzy fluorescent pink and green sneakers with jeans, and she often shared appropriate adventures from her life. Molly liked Prue a lot, in fact she was totally in love with her, but she was banging in a rhythm now, she had the rhythm down, and the impact of the wall on her head was reverberating through her head in a nourishing way.

'Molly,' Prue said. 'Molly, I have to be very clear with you, because I respect you. We all do. As you know we respect you as a person and we expect the same respect from you in return.'

This kind of talk made Molly aware of herself. She stopped banging. She was aware of herself as a lump against the wall although it was also true she was falling, falling sharply down. She took a deep breath because she thought she'd throw up.

'That's good Molly,' Prue said. 'Thank you, good choice. Now come and choose yourself something from the box, and check in.'

Molly stood up, deeply hiding her face. It hurt to show it because of the way it now looked. Whatever was happening to her was something deep inside but it was also in the process of making its way out.

Molly moved towards Prue. Prue lifted the lid of the box, which was not a box at all, it was simply a transparent plastic storage container that had a piece of thick masking tape stuck across the side. Someone had written the words 'Self Soothe' on the tape. Molly recalled a similar box she once had, marked 'Memories'. She looked inside. The room was pulsing past her peripheral point of view and she felt a certain throbbing in her teeth which meant one thing. However, the objects in the container came through to her fairly clearly: a Rubik's cube; a rubber orange bouncy ball, covered with spikes; a small plush purple heart; some kind of plush bear on the end of a key chain which Molly knew, if she pulled the tail, would begin to shake. She chose the Rubik's cube and took her place on the chair.

'Great choice Molly,' Prue said, moving her sneakers up and down. 'How are you today? What's been going on?'

'I'm terrific,' Molly said. 'There is nothing wrong with me.'

She heard Florence grunt and shift in her chair and she knew if she turned to look at her she'd see the craters on her chin. There was something about her, Molly thought, she was her or she was she. This was just the kind of knowledge making itself known to her at the time.

'I don't mean there is nothing wrong with me, exactly,' Molly said. 'I mean I believe I have a lot of problems with my behaviour, I know. And my thinking. What I mean to say is, like, you know, I have no decent excuse. Nothing bad has ever happened to me.'

Her stomach turned and a rush of heat came over her. Sweat began to drip into the small of her back and she could feel her upper arms buzz and the sides of her head buzz as well.

'Everybody else here has a decent excuse,' Molly said. 'I've got no excuse. I wasn't abused as a kid. There is no reason for me to be here. I wasn't hurt. I wasn't raped.'

Prue nodded, openly thinking this through. Her eyes were two pools of mud in an otherwise milk-bottle face.

'Well as you know Molly,' she said, 'we have a strictly non-judgmental approach at this hospital.'

She brought her hands together in the way people do when they pray and she pointed her fingers at Molly as she spoke – for sincerity, Molly guessed, and also emphasis. It was dangerous when she switched this way, to collective first.

'It's vital we accept ourselves for where we are now,' Prue said. 'Let's not increase our suffering by judging too much.'

As Prue talked, Molly felt the bodies on the chairs around her as her disgusting own – Florence's craters, Suzanne's lips, the breasts on the girl to her left which sat squarely on her stomach, glum. Molly felt her fingers pulsing with those impressive breasts, growing wide and wet and thick, and she curled her fingers tighter around the Rubik's cube for calm. *Calm*, she squeezed the cube. *There was nothing for the calm.*

Prue went on, oblivious to all of this.

'There are two minutes left for your check-in session,' she said, 'and we want you to make the most of your time with us today. How have you been managing the night-time activities? How has the mindfulness been going?'

There was no clock in the room but something started to tick. The hard corners of the cube were cool under Molly's thumb and she had a vision of launching it at Prue's bobbing head as the empty words discharged from her small, pretty mouth. Prue went on talking this way until Molly's two minutes was up. And then she moved on to the owner of the unhappy breasts.

Molly still thinks of those days. That was twelve years ago. She thinks of them while she's working, while she's shopping online. She thinks of them walking home from her ordinary office life. What she is thinking is not clear or complete. It has something to do with the girls and something to do with the trees.

When she thinks of them now they're still sitting at lunch. They ate lunch at a picnic table on the balcony overlooking the drive. The hospital served cold shiny chicken, shredded lettuce, white bread. Boiled eggs, pre-peeled, grey and curled at the tips. The eating was a special time, each girl's head bent low to her pale, piled plate as she worked her mouth in jagged circles, around and around. It was so quiet! At the end of the driveway were the hospital gates which Molly couldn't see through but she could see over. Now and then as she ate Molly looked up, expecting leaves, but all she could see were the brittle twisted tops of the trees and the tops of the trucks and the buses going by on Franklin Street. She wanted to do something, or say something, for everyone. But she swallowed her egg like everyone else. In this way another lunchtime came and stayed and was gone.

There was a Man Screaming on Broadway

There was a man screaming on Broadway. He was walking quite fast and high up on his toes. I was crossing the road with two steamed buns in my hand. Correction: one bun was in my hand, the other was in my mouth. Not all the way inside but well on its way when the man screamed again.

'Jaycee! Jayy-cee!'

As the man passed me he thumped himself twice in the head. He screamed again. I turned around. Then he sat down quietly with his legs crossed on the footpath outside the church.

At the bus stop I sat down to wait. It was hot and the sky was blue and the sun was in my eyes. As a rule I stand up when I wait for the bus but I'd been up since a quarter past four and it was now three o'clock. My desk in the office was right under the air-conditioning vent, I'd been freezing cold all day, so I sat down in the sun.

Another man came along. He had the longest dreadlocks I have ever seen. He leaned up against the glass frame of the bus shelter and dropped his backpack onto the ground at his feet. He had on a green t-shirt and a pair of black tracksuit pants with holes in them. He wore a baseball cap and his sneakers were unlaced and his face was all messed up so you could tell that he was homeless, or in some other kind of bad shape. At first he just stood there but then he turned his whole body the other way and that's how come I noticed his arm.

Now the thing to say about that arm is that there was no hand at the end of it. It had been chopped off, just above the elbow. Possibly some surgeon had saved this guy's life somewhere along the line by taking his arm? Or maybe he'd been born with one good arm and messed up his bad arm in some kind of a brawl. Or maybe the arm had been stood on by a horse. Or perhaps it was involved in a lawnmower accident caused by his father when this guy was two years old. I didn't want to look. But then I did. The arm was thick with scars, and the scars were stretched across the bone. It was just there, sticking out of his green t-shirt and the sleeve of his t-shirt was flapping about in a demented way in the breeze. I tried to think of other things but I was worried that this guy might get on my bus. Sure enough, when the bus came, he climbed on after me. I had a choice to make, and fast.

As a rule, I never sit down in the open seating section at the front of a bus. This is because you have to face people. Also, there is the matter of mothers and their prams. Once I was on a full bus when this mother with a pram made to get on the bus. Ma'am, the next bus, the bus driver said. Just behind me, I'm full. He was very sweet, this bus driver, the way he said that. Maybe he hadn't even noticed it had sort of started raining? The mother was beside herself. What? the mother screamed. You're gonna let these fucken cunts on the bus? I've got a baby here! The bus driver immediately noticed his mistake. Sorry, ma'am, he said. I'm sorry. Come on. But the mother didn't come. She was very upset. We were all fucken cunts, in her personal opinion, who wouldn't let a mother and her baby on the bus. I was sitting in the open seating section, watching all this play out, and I was tempted to feel like a cunt myself when she put it like that. I looked at all the other people sitting in the open seating section of the bus. They weren't cunts at all, I thought, only people.

I never wanted to put myself in that kind of position again. But I was tired, I'd been cold all day and now I was hot because I had made the mistake of sitting in the sun. As the bus pulled away I sat down in the first empty seat, which was in the open seating section of the bus.

There was a seat free next to me and the guy could have sat down. I wasn't taking his seat. He could have sat down next to me anytime he liked. Instead he stood up in the aisle. It was his prerogative to do this and he did it. His cap was pulled down lower now. He leaned against the pole and his backpack rested against his leg. The pack was open and, as the bus paused at the lights, he bent down to collect something from inside. He produced a grey plastic shopping bag, stood up straight and passed the bag to his other arm, the arm where the other hand should have been.

He didn't let the bag go right away. The receiving arm had no hand at the end of it and no fingers with which to take the bag. But the stump of his arm looked all set to take it. I don't know how I could tell this but it looked primed. Perhaps its end poked a little further out of his green t-shirt. Or did it wriggle around? Not wriggling, exactly, for that gives one the idea of fingers or worms, but it was sort of shifting about freely, sort of side to side to side. Anyway, so this guy, he took his hand away. And the plastic bag stayed put, held by the stump somehow, like magic.

Now I have my own ideas about amputated limbs and plastic bags. Generally, I think that if you have an amputated limb it is for a good reason, that the limb has no intention of behaving like an ordinary limb and you shouldn't make it. Added to this you should not do any tricks. I didn't like what this guy was doing with his stump. It seemed a trick to me, the way he held that bag, sort of floating in a special way all about his stump. Plus, now I could smell him. I think it was his hair. The bus lurched to a stop outside the Golden Fang and this guy lost his footing and I got a big whiff. He regained his balance and the plastic bag made a significant shift, but he never dropped it. From what I could tell he made a sort of awkward shrugging motion with his shoulder to keep a hold on the bag. I would have preferred him not to struggle like that, with the bag and also with his footing. Honestly I thought it would really have been best he had not got on the bus at all for it was so unpleasant to sit there like that, facing him and his situation. So I said: 'Would you like to sit down?'

'No thanks,' he said.

The doors hissed closed and we made our way along the road. I didn't want to continue watching him but now I couldn't avoid it. He slipped around on account of the natural motions of the bus then started digging around inside the backpack again. This time he produced coins. He dropped these coins in the plastic bag. He repeated this process several times, shovelling for the coins and then reaching across himself and letting them go in the bag. When he was finished, he took the bag off his stump and put it in his pack. Then he made for the seat next to me and sat down.

I didn't want to be sitting next to him. He was a homeless guy, he had some bad situation with his arm, the laces on his sneakers were undone and he did not smell okay. I did not appreciate the way his thigh was touching my thigh. Or how close our bodies were pressed together in the open seating section of the bus. I didn't like it but I recognised that it would have been a very bad thing to stand up. I couldn't stand up without making my feelings clear so I just sat there trying hard not to feel anything.

The thing was his good arm was next to me. I'm not saying I appreciated his arm pressed up against my arm like that, his thigh on my thigh – not by any means – but if I had to choose an arm to be pressed up against my arm I would rather that one so I tried to be glad. The bus pulled up at the stop outside the university. A flock of Transport Officers were waiting there, ready to get on.

When I saw the Transport Officers I got a little worried. I still didn't have a card but I knew just the kind of look to arrange on my face. They got on the bus, each with their special bum bags and their button-up shirts. One short, round one came up to me. When he asked for my card and I shook my head he grew serious with me.

'I'm sorry,' I said. 'I left my wallet at work.'

'Is this your first offence?' he said.

'Oh, yes,' I said.

'I'll need your name and address.'

I recited these.

'You're in the system,' he said. 'If you get caught without your card again you'll get a fine.'

'Okay,' I said. 'Thank you very much.'

The Transport Officer turned to the guy next to me and held out his hand.

'Oh no,' the guy said. 'I don't have one yet.'

He unzipped his backpack and produced a bunch of coins.

'I can pay,' the guy said.

'You'll need to step off the bus.'

'I have to be somewhere.'

'Please, sir. Step off the bus.'

When the doors hissed closed and the bus pulled away, I stood up and looked back. The guy was standing there at the bus stop. The Transport Officers were talking to each other, acting like he wasn't there. The guy waited a second longer and then he walked off. He stood there at the crossing, waiting to cross, and as our light went green his light went green too so I had a very good view of his bad arm. I turned my head as the bus drew along just in time to see the stump give a small, sad, dignified little wave. I thought how cruel it was, taking a guy off a bus. But then the bus passed him, and I was on it.

You and Everyone You Know

Trenton was drinking beer and eating potato chips and watching a program about the Tudors. He had tuned in just in time to hear how they put hooks in the babies to bring them out if the pushing wasn't working – forceps hadn't been invented. He thought this was the last thing he needed to hear. But he kept the program on since it was either that, or a show about amphibians.

Nothing interested him as he watched, even though many interesting things took place. Anne died suddenly. And Henry had a lot of wardrobe changes. Trenton drank beer and ate potato chips and thought how completely he wanted a body to love. It seemed a simple thing. He was too scared to try a brothel. He got to thinking: in six hundred years' time, no-one would be sitting around watching a program about how he died, or talking about what clothes he wore, or what he liked to do with his current wife's head whenever he felt like it. He looked down at himself. He was wearing black pants and a yellow t-shirt. He didn't have a wife.

The next program was called *Top Ten Far Out Things*. He learned something: his chances of dying suddenly without any interference from the outside world were one in 200,000. This chance was increased by a macronaut every thousand bananas he ate. He didn't know what a macronaut was but he'd eaten a lot of bananas. When he was small, according to his mother, he would wake in his white wooden cot and hold onto the bars and demand a banana until she appeared with one. He had no memory, himself, of the banana first thing. It was his mother's memory and he felt it shouldn't be inside of him, along with the part where she would carry him still sleeping into her bed, lay his head on the pillow and kiss him full on the lips. He could not recall this, exactly, but he felt it somewhere, his mother loving him in a desperate, frantic way that smelled like soft fruit and didn't mean anything.

Another *Far Out Thing* was celery. You burned more calories eating celery than the celery actually contained. He wanted to love a soft body. He wanted to do it from behind. He felt a turn in his throat and got up for more beer.

No, he would not cry. When he opened the beer at the bench he thought hard on the body, on its pinkness, its width, its texture, its shape. He would like to grip her shoulder, even dig his nails in. He kept fine nails. He sat back down with his beer and kept his eyes on the screen.

There was only one vegetarian spider on earth, this was another *Far Out Thing*. Trenton swallowed hard and pinched his nose. It was something a child might do underwater. Lately Trenton had been feeling unwell. His jaw ached and although he was very tired, when he lay down he couldn't sleep. Or rather he could sleep but the dreams he had were perverse. He kept dreaming of a big, red penis on a very big man. In the dream the penis surprised him, and he handled it with both hands like a musical instrument. The big man looked down at him, neither amused nor alarmed. In the dream Trenton thought vaguely of a giant, a vegetable and a bird; it excited him and he turned around, bent over and immediately woke up. After these dreams he was dizzy, like he was spinning. The only things that helped were eating or drinking something, or pacing around. He switched off the television and got up and did a lap of the house fast. Then he finished his beer at the bench. He was drunk, it would help to go for a walk, take a shower, drink some water, go to bed. Or he might forget the shower and go directly to bed. Wake up in the morning and try again.

It was a hot night, nearly summer, but the wind was strong and as he walked he felt better. He thought perhaps he should move to the beach. There was always a wind at the beach, a wind that seemed to say something good was on its way. What was the point in staying here? He'd live some place he could smell the salt and hear the sea at night. He would move some place where, in the winter, he could sit alone on the rocks by the sea and see the whole grey world, still and absent, all set out before him for a long, long time.

There were one or two cars but otherwise it was quiet, except for the wind bringing summer. There were a number of ghost gums, wide at the lower trunk where the bark hung off in sheets. One of the trees was distorted near the top where two round bulbs like great breasts protruded before the limbs and leaves branched out, for the head. Trenton stopped in front of this one tree and looked up. Then he ran his open palm across the skin of the trunk and pressed his cheek to it.

He knew these trees but he'd never seen them this way before. He put his arms around the tree. He looked up at her branches, which were rushing with leaves. He closed his eyes. The hard cool trunk, rough in places, pressed against the soft skin of his inner upper arm and he thought that's how all lovers start, with the insides of the outsides and then they work their way in. The number 200,000 swirled rivers in his head. He thought he would come. He thought he'd be sick. He thought he heard screaming. Wait, yes — someone screamed.

Trenton began to jog along the footpath. Then he started to run. He ran to the church and through the side gate into the cemetery.

A girl was lying naked under a banksia tree. Her clothes were on the grass. A man was standing over her, also naked, and he seemed to Trenton to be in a position of extreme uncertainty. His penis glanced off to the side. The girl writhed on the grass but it wasn't a happy writhe.

The man looked up. His skin was completely black and now his teeth were pure white. He did not attempt to hide his nakedness. His nipples were large and quiet and he merely looked from Trenton to the girl on the ground. The girl had long, pale legs which she was pedalling in the air. Her legs came to a point at her pink pubic hair. Trenton had never seen anything like it.

'Is everything okay?' Trenton said. 'I thought I heard a scream.'

'Praising,' the man said.

In the church, someone screamed.

'As you can see,' the man said, 'we are having ourselves a situation here.'

As the girl pedalled the air more voices rang out from the church. There was music, there was language, and now and then someone screamed. The man began to laugh, a bold and broken thing, he laughed so hard he had to lean on the gate and Trenton took the chance to take in the girl's breasts, which sank to the side every time she moved and sprang up again when she grew still.

When Trenton got home he opened another beer. He sat on the steps, thinking he was all right. It was true, he was thinking, he didn't have anybody to love – that everyone he'd ever loved was in love with somebody else. But it was also true he was young and his whole life was in front of him. It came to him things could be worse. He could be crazy or dead. People were always getting killed by cancers or viruses or cars or themselves and buried behind some church and he thought, it will happen to you too, it will happen to you and everyone you know. He was thinking he'd led such a sheltered life, his mother was the roof of that life and he was inside it, his mother was the front door of that life and the walls and the floor. He was inside that life and he had to get out. Oh, he wished he was gay! He knew of a place where you paid an entrance fee and just like that you were in. Perhaps he wanted filling? Pounding, inside. Perhaps *he* wanted a hand on *his* shoulder with nails bearing down and a hot, strong tongue stabbing between his teeth. Yes, perhaps *he* wanted fucking. He drank his beer and considered it.

Nothing in the Night

The boy is running again. You can tell by his feet that's what he is doing. The curtain over the front window shifts, as if I've created some breeze. Beyond the curtain the day is turning on. The mynahs call out, loud and sure and hurt, and the boy appears back and forth inside the window frame, and he is running.

The first time I saw him he was outside a different window. As far as I could tell all he was doing was running down to the bottom of the driveway and back up. The thing was I couldn't see his whole self all that well because between the window where I was and the running boy there was a fence. The fence belonged to both of us but the fence was falling down. So the first I saw of the boy, if I can strip it right back, was his straight black hair as it flicked up and down above the fence. His hair was fairly short but not short enough that it couldn't lift off his head like a billion tiny hands, waving at me. He was small, I'll say that. The t-shirt he wore was too big.

This was yesterday, the day my wife up and died. She was in the bedroom eating a bowl of muesli because she knew how much the spoon smacking on the edge of the porcelain disturbed me when I worked. I was standing at the kitchen window, washing up a glass. Seeing the boy's hair wave alarmed me and in response I dropped the glass. My wife came out of the window, screaming. This confused me. I wanted to tell her a boy was out there. I said I would take care of the glass.

When I looked for him the boy was gone. I sat down to work. But then I put the pencil down because I remembered the glass. I went back into the kitchen to take care of it but then my wife called out, one last time, from the bed. When I got in there she was already dead. I got into the bed and curled around her. It was kind of amazing to think that if I didn't call the ambulance immediately I'd be sleeping with my wife dead in my arms, voluntarily. I had a choice to make. But I couldn't make the choice. So I got out of the bed and

I went back to the kitchen and sat down to work. With my wife dead in the next room – dead, yes, but still there.

I don't mind saying I was dying then as well. I'm sick with something rare – I've got this dizziness and I keep losing things. I've lost so much this year: my reading glasses, six hundred dollars cash, one cat with a distinctive black mark on her nose. Take the actual time to ask me how it feels and I'll tell you it's like two large, black hands about the brain. Squeezing. Applying this unbelievable pressure in my skull so the pain drips thickly down. I was dying the first time I saw the running boy and I am dying now as I look at him running out the front.

I open the front door and walk out onto the veranda. I stand there with one hand on the railing looking at the steps, which I mean to go down, but every time I move my feet the running boy comes along and I have to pause and look up. I'll say something this time, that's what I'll do. I'll say something to him while I still have the time. But the hands squeeze inside, claiming the space in my head, absolving me of a certain responsibility. To speak to him. To tell him something concrete. But the hands squeeze, they're made of nothing, but they'll be the end of me.

His steps make that crucial flat smacking sound as he runs, and those fine black hairs lift well clear of his head. They rise and fall in a tremendous, friendly way. I'd like to move my neck to look around, to look better at the boy, but the fingers, at the tips, are jet cool on my spine and I can't move my neck for what the fingers might do. So I just stand right here, one hand on the railing, my wife dead in the next room beating out the porcelain time.

We didn't meet at the beginning, my wife and I. We made this life together. We lived inside of that. We had to go on some crazy long time past the normal end, past ordinary. It was crazy when we met, it was crazy when we made him, it was crazy when we left him. It was crazy we had a party and buried him in the yard. We planted marigolds on top but my wife changed her mind in the middle of the night and we drew back the dirt with our fingers, our nails, then we set him between us in the box, in the bed.

And my wife felt better.

But the next morning I told her, you better get some help. I drove her to the beach. She looked out at the grey ocean, all foam and tips. He was the greatest thing that ever happened to me, she said, and I don't know his name. She screwed up her fists and rained them down on her thighs. His name was Ben, I said. We named him Benjamin. She put her head into the headrest fast, five hundred times.

In any case now I've got a clear view of the boy. He's really running. From this angle I can see exactly what he does, how he runs to the end of the street and hits the trunk of a white ghost gum with his hand and runs back, passing but not acknowledging me. If anything, as he comes closer, he puts his head further down. I can see close up like this how wet his t-shirt is. There's liquid pouring from his head and this sticks his t-shirt down and his hair at the back is pressed down as well. I wonder where a mother could find a pink t-shirt like that. Perhaps it got that way in the wash.

Now he runs past the banksia tree. He runs with his chest puffed way out and his arms working hard in a way that isn't neat, that isn't natural, like it is some great effort for him to move through the air. He will soon enough drown, I know, doing it that way. I put one foot on the stairs because he's disappeared again. But now I can hear, yes here he comes, one small steady smack on the concrete, then the next.

I don't recall anything sharp about the way I got down but I know I must have done it because I'm standing at the gate. Half the brick wall is to my right and the other half is to my left and I am right in the middle. I never thought a gate would benefit me this way. The gate is an old fashioned one, it came with the house, and now I wrap both hands around the iron at the top, to prop me up. The hands apply the pressure deep inside my head so the hurt drips down as far as my right hip bone and stops. I have it in my head to go further out and lie down. I could go through the gate if I could open it all the way and then I could lie down in the middle of the street and wait for a car to come along and that would be the death of me. It would be something, at least, to end things that way. Not this disaster.

The iron of the gate is cool and damp from the night and I remember exactly this place on the wall because this was the part of the wall where I couldn't balance any books. When my wife left me the first time I thought I'd get rid of all our books. They were balanced either side of the gate, one on top of the next up to four, all arranged alphabetically. I carried them out in a bag. I did this over two trips. I set all those books up along the brick fence, A to L on one side of the gate and M to Z on the other. Then I went inside to see what would happen next.

An old man, stooped over in a long jacket, came along. He picked up my collector's edition *Grapes of Wrath*. I'd never read it to the end but as I watched him turn it over in his twisted hands I remembered my wife giving it to me. I held onto the curtains and watched this bastard turn page after page. He took his time. I honestly thought he would steal my favourite book. Then he put the book down, and walked away. I dragged the bag back out the front and pushed it up against the wall. I swept the books back in, armful at a time, and whichever books didn't quite make it in I considered a sign and took them down to the Christian Care shop. But that was only a game I played. The next day I went straight down and bought all the books back.

There is no sign of the boy. I've forgotten him again. Perhaps he's changed his plan, perhaps he's given up, perhaps he's gone down the other end of the street and he's looping around and then he'll come back this way. The midsummer air is cold on my teeth and nearly everywhere you go in our street, this time of day, a car door slams. The light is too deep and too bright like a thumb tip between the brows pressing hard in your sleep and then the boy appears again as if he never went away. He runs past me from the direction of the driveway which belongs to the house where his family might live. I'm thinking he belongs to the woman in the glass. She stands in the kitchen, in the middle of the frame, holding a bottle of green liquid in her brittle blue hands.

The boy runs my way. Now he looks up at me. That's a shock. He looks me square in the face and his eyes are very open but they don't expect a thing from me, they simply look. The closer he gets the more I can see. Yes, his skin is very gold, that's still true, but from under his hairline there are blessings of water running over two temples. When he puts his head down and runs past me I can see those diamonds making glass crumbs in a trail along his neck. I prepare myself to tell this to him, but then I change my mind. Something more urgent to say comes to me and I have to speak out. I grip the iron of the gate with my fingers made of ice. That's not running, I say. Whatever it is you think you're doing, that's not running. Then I remember that these aren't my words. I read them somewhere and they don't belong to me. They're in my head and in my hips and in my blood and in my teeth but whatever I say it won't change anything.

She said this to me under the Moreton Bay Fig where we buried him finally. She said she understood that words wouldn't change anything but it was also true that she could finally say what was wrong. He was the biggest thing that ever happened to me, she said, and he never happened. The biggest thing that ever happened to me never happened to me at all. I considered what she said and I had to disagree. He happened, I said. He's still happening.

Look how he runs, how he shuffles his feet. And his chest, the way it puffs out, breaking out of his front ribs and arriving everywhere first. His elbows are bent but not bent all the way. His arms are working the air at his sides but he'll drown, he'll surely drown, doing it that way. I push off the gate, intending to shout out. I plan to give it to him simple and straight. That's not running, I'll say. Hey, whatever you think you're doing, that's not running!

But the cold air pushes in, full of fresh dirt, and I can hear my wife working at the lock on the door. The sun is coming up, it's slashing through the trees. And there are slips of red hair from the banksia trees all over the pavement where the boy runs, back and forth, and stops running.

I didn't make the choice to leave anywhere but I am well through the gate when the sky turns to red. Now and then my wife turns the key. But apart from that sound which came to me, nothing in the night moved at all.

I am Here Today to Talk to You about Surprises

There have been three great surprises in my life. And when I think about these surprises my heart shouts and electricity in the shape and style of jelly beans charges through my bones. I am talking about the expensive jelly beans, too, violet coloured and spotted like garden frogs with an exotic disease.

I don't want to spend too much time on the first surprise. It happened in childhood, okay? I want to tell you about the most recent surprise when the police showed up at my place.

They buzzed.
    When I accepted the buzz, I knew what it was about.
    'Okay, okay,' I said. Then I might have gone: 'Grrr.'
    Like the police buzzing me was some big inconvenience.

I pressed the button to let them in and opened the door. I was in the short shorts and t-shirt I sleep and work in.
    'Hello,' one of them said. She had dark hair. 'We are here to…'
    'Come in, come in, come in,' I said. 'Or else everyone will hear.'
    They entered. They did it slowly, like they were skating on ice.

'I am sorry there is nowhere to sit,' I said.
    In truth there was one chair and one wooden stool. The stool I made myself when I was seventeen.
    'You can sit there and there,' I said, indicating these items.
    'It's fine,' the blonde one said. 'You make yourself comfortable.'

I sat down on the hard cushion I write on, on the floor. I had a book on the floor in front of me, and a notebook, and a little pencil.
    'What are you reading?' the dark one said, picking up the book.

'It's poetry,' I said.

She flicked through the book, then studied the author's photograph on the cover.

'I think I've heard of him,' she said.

'She's a woman,' I said. 'A they now, actually. Yes.'

There was a bit of silence. But it was a special silence because it involved the police. They had all their appendages. They had their blue shirts. They had their hair very neat, they had their black boots and their batons and their torches and their guns.

'You've got a lovely place here,' the dark one said, laying down the book. She put her hands on her knees and leant in towards me, looking directly into my face.

'It's very small,' I said. 'I'm sorry there's nowhere to sit.'

'It's fine,' the blonde one said. 'You should see some of the places we go. Poo in the corner, needles everywhere.' Then she got down on her knees, sat back on her heels. 'You can tell it's clean if I'm sitting on the floor,' she said.

'You know who you look like?' the dark one said.

She got her phone out.

All my life people have been telling me who I look like. I used to find this weirdly comforting. Like maybe I didn't have to be myself at all, perhaps I could be one person or the next. Or maybe my looking like all these different people was some indication of my inextricable connection to the human race. But lately I've decided what I'd really like is to look just like myself and nobody else. Built like a loaf of brown bread and looking good in red lipstick. And a black and white dress.

'Honestly,' the dark one said, 'America Ferrera. You look like America Ferrera.'

She turned her phone to me and I had a look. She turned her phone to the blonde police officer.

'I can see the resemblance,' she said.

Since the police buzzed on my door and spent some significant time with me inside my flat, it's like anything can happen here and maybe it will. It's opened up a realm. Like when your mother tries to kill herself, that opens up a realm. Suddenly everything is on the table – suddenly everything is a distinct possibility, there aren't any rules and all bets are off.

Or is it that nobody is placing bets anymore?

Or is it that there are still plenty of people placing bets, it's just the horses are not even remotely aware they are racing towards a future where their legs will be turned into glue sticks small enough to be manipulated by tiny hands, and their bright satin sashes sent to an orphanage in Nepal to be turned into sanitary products in the name of sustainability?

The blonde one was kneeling on the floor. The dark haired one was standing up. She put her phone away. I put my head down and cried.

'It's good to have a good cry, get it out,' the dark one said. 'I admit I have my days when I cry as well. It's good to have a good cry. That's all right.'

I could feel the blonde one nodding, her face all gorgeous and concerned.

'I need to get socks,' I said. 'I need underwear.'

'Is it okay if I check the drawer for weapons?' the blonde one said. 'I need to make sure there is nothing in there that could hurt you or us.'

What an exceptional thing are young women today. I admire them tremendously, with their protocol and their kind faces. And how do police officers get such shiny hair? Then it occurred to me. The day of the month. And as it occurred to me I felt the rush of blood.

'Oh my god,' I said. 'I'm getting my period. I need to go to the bathroom.'

'Okay,' the dark one said.

Then she went into the bathroom.

'There's a razor in the shower,' I said. 'There are tweezers on the shelf.'

'Thank you,' she said.

'Please leave the door open,' the blonde one said. Then: 'We'll turn around.'

'Thank you,' I said.

Once, when I was in high school, I had to change my tampon by the side of the road. I did this behind somebody's boat parked in the drive. It was either that, or turn up to school in a bloodied dress. I thought that was my best tampon tale.

'Are you all right?' the dark one said.

'I'm all right,' I said.

I thought about throwing myself up against the wall, pounding my head out of consciousness, killing myself there and then through sheer animal force. But instead I finished the job, washed my hands, and emerged.

'What else?' the blonde one said. 'We'll get it for you.'

'It's easier,' the dark one said. 'Plus, we want to help.'

So then I stood in my flat directing the help.

'The deodorant is in that cupboard. Yes, that one,' I said.

'The shoes are in the wardrobe. Not those ones!' I said.

And in this manner the police officers helped me get dressed.

They were unspeakably respectful. They did not express any alarm that the socks and the underwear are kept in the kitchen drawers, the deodorant above the oven next to the olive oil.

But this is such a small flat! I did not think to protest. There are other things I want to tell them, from this distance. Like how it was such a surprise, them turning up just like that.

The moral of this story is that it's better to wait around for some surprise to happen in your life than it is to commit suicide, even if the surprises are very few and the waiting is very hard.

You can do things while you wait. Like Google, 'How to spell Napal.' Or eat a Neapolitan ice cream. Or fight a Neapolitan war.

My advice? It is good to avoid Provence — take a route through the Alps. Insert your tampon, sugar. Then rip open your coat.

Honey

My girlfriend says that the first time she met me she thought, well that's a ride I want to get on. When I tell her someone I once loved said my voice was like honey my girlfriend says, oh yes honey – honey, honey, honey. She makes love to me while I'm sitting at my desk. She makes love to me at exactly nine o'clock on a Saturday night on my hardwood floor while the fireworks go off over the harbour. The fireworks are back and my girlfriend says, I was right you are a ride but you're such a gentle ride and I never want to get off. I have plain hair and it's grey at the temples. I bite my nails and spit them out and pick my nose and play with it. I have howled in public places for the last twenty years and I have wanted to die over and over again. I have chicken skin on the backs of my thighs and I'm prone to weight gain, I rarely lose. Haha, my girlfriend says. Hahahaha. Keep going, she says. We're just getting started here.

We are just getting started in this relationship. In the morning, on the bed, while the dog tip taps across the floorboards anticipating his breakfast, my girlfriend runs her hand up and down the length of my thigh. She turns her palm down, then flips her hand, then turns the palm down again as she moves it up and down like she's conducting. Her hand doesn't lose contact with my skin at any stage. She is talking about her work. She had a guy who died recently of septicaemia. Another one of heartbreak. He lost his dog in the night and had a fall in the street. She attended him. He was crying for his dog but she put him in her truck. She had to do it. She felt so for him. He died shortly before dawn, about the same time a nurse found the dog sitting quietly outside the entrance to Emergency. He was ninety-six years old, my girlfriend says, but there were no obvious injuries. Now the dog tip taps around my bed. We have been feeding him toast with marmalade, dripping with butter. We cut the crusts off because he has very few teeth.

When my girlfriend is at work I am at work, too. My girlfriend is dealing with life and death. I am dealing with no such thing. I interview people for a living and then write up reports. I talk to my colleague about his romances, about his new exercise regime. I tell him about my girlfriend, about how good she is. Plus she looks so cute, I say, in her navy uniform. I iron her uniform with extreme pride like I am a real wife.

Some days we go ten, twelve hours without any contact at all. I practice my breathing, knowing she will return. Knowing some days she will wait for me outside my office building, knowing she'll put a hand either side of my face, right where we are, and kiss me on the lips. Then she'll take my hand and lock the fingers into hers. Sometimes she'll kiss my hand before she lets it drop. Our arms swing together as we walk. We'll walk down to my place or her place, or the supermarket. This is the life we have imagined for ourselves. Now we are making it. There is no template for this love. If there is, I haven't seen it.

Sometimes, when my girlfriend works late, she'll come over unannounced. Maybe she's had a bad shift, or maybe she just wants to see me. Maybe it's the little dog we've finally called Joe. Joe seems to have forgotten his old life. He seems, now, entirely mixed up with us. We'll both be sleeping when she arrives. Joe in his bed. Me in mine. She'll let herself in. I'll hear it as if in a dream. She'll take a long shower in my bathroom. Then she'll dry herself too quickly, drop the towel on the floor and get in bed, behind me. For a moment I'll be completely awake. I love you, I'll say. I love you, she'll say. She'll wrap one arm around my middle, tuck the tips of her fingers underneath my waist. The other arm she'll slip fully underneath me – I don't know how she does it, she is an expert at this. I am not a small woman, but she holds me easily. My legs will be curled up in sleep. She'll fit her knees behind my knees and we'll fall asleep like this. Although I am asleep, I can feel her breath on the back of my neck, the soft pressure of her nose, and the cold wisps of her hair that are still completely wet.

I wake to my alarm and Joe scratching on the floorboards. He does this urgently, with just the one paw. This is his language for breakfast. I feed him.

I shower and get dressed. I make a pot of coffee and put my make-up on and do my hair and, many, many times I look at her in the bed. She sleeps like a creature too brave for this place. She is not a large person, her skin is so pale, and her hair spreads out in long, dark rivers along the pillow. She stops breathing sometimes. Then she takes a big dramatic breath. She blows it out like bubbles. Then she is quiet again. I sit down on the bed. Darling, I say, kissing her closed eyes. One, then the next. I wake her this way. Darling, I say. Darling. It's the day.

Over coffee we make plans. Dinner, the weekend. She wants to visit her best friend in the country next month. We'll need to hire a car. Joe eats his marmalade toast. He drinks from his bowl. Every time he does this we both fall silent and watch. His music with the water is different to the music of the rain. I tell her this. She agrees. She reaches for me, says my name. I am getting these things down because they are the ordinary movements of our day. And they amaze me.

Later, my girlfriend will tell me everything she saw on the road, in the houses, in Emergency. She'll tell me all the decisions she made and what she now thinks of these decisions. She plays everything out. When she is finished, she smiles. She moves on to the next thing. And what did you write yesterday? she says. Can I hear it? Not yet, I say. I've got to go through it one more time. She pulls me down on her lap and kisses me.

Roar

Roar. Raw. Root. Reckon. Reek. Reign. Rough. Roar. I am howling for you. I am here on the precipice. I am at the cliff face. I am calling for you.

My mouth is open. The salt water pours in. I swallow like an ancient frog as big as the world. As fat as Neptune. As wide as outer space. How long is a light year today? We are fairly confident it is only one hundred to one fifty light years across. It is not made of nothing. Is it a hard vacuum? And what is so hard about it?

My body draws back like a corridor in a house built of plasma between galaxies, dark matter millions of kelvins hot. G-forces are never exactly zero. Travelling far enough into deep space to reduce the effect of gravity by attenuation to zero is possible but highly impractical and requires travelling a very large distance. For example, to reduce the gravity of the Sun by even a factor of one million you have to move roughly three point one seven billion kilometres away. However, it is worth acknowledging that the gravity on Earth, thanks to the Milky Way, is already attenuated by a factor greater than one million so we don't need to go anywhere and we don't need a coat. A coat hangs on the door. A scarf hangs. A body.

II

I still recall her speech on black holes. It was amazing. She could always tempt me and she had a music about her. I was slowing with the letters. I was speeding up. She was a woman. They did not invite the parents. There was no mother and no dad. There were no witnesses to what took place. She looked like her and I. She looked like one of us. She was plenty prettier. Far. Attractive and interested in commodities I had never considered before. Her interest in heliopauses was a growth. Black holes were for babies, she said. Black holes were for blurbs. This was the real substance. The extraordinary principle of science and the manifestation of deep time.

She looked very good in her blue sweater and her blue scarf. Always blue. Blue is a colour and a condition. Blue is a disease and a dictionary of plaintive terms. Lexical was not a statement. A map was not a page. Blue is a sweater and a pair of lips and a scarf, which, quite incredibly, she hung herself with on the back of the door to her flat in kind of amazing fashion in 1963.

Anyway I was born. She many years before and also later. We were born in circles, her and I. Our birth was a synapse. We qualified. We were a venture. We were an amusement park. We were an anomaly. Nothing special. Nothing far out. It wasn't the sixties. It was too early for that. It was the premi-60s. We were not merchandise. I wanted to get her thoughts on the cluster. And I wanted the cluster to explode. And I wished for her to explain it to me. I wanted to line up all the lines, embrace their curves, append and appease them; weather. We were not joined in a conscionable manner but we were related. We were related, related – distant realities. Distant galaxies. I mean nobody told me it would rain today. It came as an amazing surprise.

I climbed the bridge. And I entered the friendship garden. And four young girls were dancing. One of them on the outside. But the gold shapes were possibly fish. And I was walking once more. And I looked up and it was dark.

III

Beyond the termination of shock is the region of the heliosphere called the heliosheath. It is amazing but not a woman. What is a year? It is planetary in scope and configuration. It is not time. Time is not language is not a principle of flight is not waiting. Is not coffee in a tiny white cup of bowel problems. She sent me a photograph called uterus long. I said thank you. The sonographer. Who used an interstellar probe to tell the story of inside which was categorically fixed to the outside but entirely separate from it so that the vision of it was possible from the outside but you couldn't reach it. Not with light years or with distance or with anything. But she had her probe. We were repeating it. It had everything been done before. It was not interstellar. We were not lunatics. We were two women. It was just a Monday. It was just a number of birthday. Go back further. Go back in months. Go back and tell me the story of what became of you/us. Of you in a blue sweater with a swell of ideas. I wanted to take you out over the sea. I wanted to drop you down the sandstone pillars and I wanted to walk with you, which means moving. I wanted the focus to be our soft bare feet on the old, old shells of the old, old oysters.

The water is clear on the rainy days. Smears of rainbows, oil, sanitary pads, whole tins of tuna. That is irony. The brown spotted fish don't move between the rocks. They just stay there. And I wanted to take you out over the oyster beds. I wanted to hold your hand and move with you deeper and deeper until we reached the bridge and then I wanted to take you under it. For friendship purposes, on a Monday. In this way I wanted to be moving with you and I wanted it to last forever and I didn't want to wait anymore. Call it a day or a week or a year or a decade: insignificant minutes. I was always waiting. And how long would it be, that I must wait for you, and where are you when you're not here?

I would not mention the diagnosis. I would not mention the condition. I would not mention the cluster the illness the disease the prospect of a name. Against you. A name doesn't change anything, she said. And you can't name a millennia except to call it that. I said, why don't you listen? To the doctors. Why don't you try? I wanted to show you everything and I wanted to point to a single star which was orange and hung up there in the black, black sky. In the end there isn't anything original to say. There is only the smashing sun.

She was born on Earth. Different country. That is the breadth of it.

What else is there?

You are at the bottom and you are at. It is not even a mystery but it pumps through everything and all the layers become crystallised configurations of an atmosphere that is not only unbreathable but also irreplaceable, which does not consist of pressure or purpose.

I would fight for your tunnels I have too many pens when I winced or jolted or inhaled deeply or held my own fingers so tight she said *excuse me*. We were two women in a room. One of us wore a coat. She had an accent this was a part of her you couldn't separate it try it if you want you can't do it like her thick hair over her sticky-out ears that was her mask's fault she lived inside of me. In these moments she was living and I was living too and she was inside of me and she was looking around. She pointed things out. She drew lines this way and that. What's that I said? I said, yes that. She showed me kidney bladder uterus fallopian tube ovary right in the right place ovary left in the right place no dominant follicle on that side they are tubes like sea creatures I paid for this bed in my head the sea creatures are orange I paid for this bed. These ones are pink but on the screen they are grey but these ones are pink exactly my pink on a day I was drowning all over again I may have to kill my mother too going all the way back my throat the black force the darkest form of light it was tender tender tender when she hurt me she said *excuse* me *excuse* me that's your bladder there thank you for that. She had blonde hair. I said thank you too.

We were two women. We were born. It was just a Monday. We were two children in the dark room. There was a curtain. We were two women. Our bodies were interested in life. The production of it. What we were doing was extremely specific. You didn't need to have feelings to match. Whoever did? We were *producers*. We were scoping the territory. We were canvassing the setting. Here and here. Here? We kicked our tiny feet in our tiny beds. Tubes and tubes. It was not geopolitical. We were on the inside. We had on our little robes. We had on our little masks. They were feeding us. We were protected. There were pieces missing. I was born with pieces missing. It was a condition of the flesh and between the legs. Nobody could handle it. I was right on the borders. You were next to me. I was condemned and I loved everywhere I went but there wasn't a form for the love or the violence that came with it, the violence that was not safe, that I directed at myself. Yes I cut the flesh yes I betrayed the body yes I managed her with fury and malice and quite possibly I killed her. Did I plan it? We did not miss our mother. Our mother was nowhere nearby. And into the darkness she shot the force of her intergalactic fury. I looked up and it was dark.

IV

We were there in that dark room together and this was the beginning. We were two women of a single gender, she was light and I was dark, of the hair, the hair has a lot to do with it. And we were creatures of myth and history. We wore no veil. We loved our mother and this love was sex. Between us, we twirled the hair of the mother who could not witness us who could not document who was a no-good archivist who could not possibly attend to us, we, who screamed, in cots and cots. And yeah we moved around but we were a little luxury. We were women and girls and children, then, and it was something to be made and it was some possibility to enter — that there was a future for us.

V

And I wanted to tell you everything. And I wanted to start with the beginning of her name. And I wanted to say what it was to stand in the carpark so late at night and see her hanging there from the limb of the naked sassafras tree. She was not a bat or a possum. I saw it, peculiarly. She was not a widget or a watch. It was not relevant how much we loved her. There was no love that could touch her. She had nothing inside of her. She was a mirage and a moment. She was incredible.

Later, I ate a large piece of blueberry pie a man in a hat heated up and the young girl behind the counter who asked about ice cream was extremely nice to me. She had blood, too. She had this substance pounding through her because she was a living being. I wanted to crawl up into this conglomeration of cells. It was only blood. It was only a scarf. It was only a door. It was only a girl. But I was with her when she bought the scarf. Red, red, she said. No, I said. Baby blue.

VI

And they are so little these days. And there is no discussion point. And there is no marker. And there is no reality. And there is no convergence. And there is no colour purple. And there is no race. And there is no gender. And there is no intercourse. And there is no structure. And there is no catastrophe. And there is no signal. And there is no sign. And there is no species. And there is no circumstance. And there is no time. And there is no methodology. And there is no formula. And there is no art. And there is no magic. And there is no illusion. And there is no horror. And there is no music. And there is no appendage, no apostrophe, no ownership, no menace, no hunger, no pride. We held her hand and we watched her colours change. We put our love onto her and she fucked us up.

VII

A star system is a small number of stars that orbit each other. It is rolling. Don't worry about it. It is nothing to the great sea and the language. It is nothing to the atmosphere. I am making myself sick here. I am totally liberated. I am bound in twine. I am choking out.

Men sit in boats on little seas. Men! They are a part of it. Where exactly *were* you? You were in a different country. You were part of the mystery. We never even met. This is technology. The sea is a very small thing. The distance is close. Call it the ocean. As a young woman I screamed for you there on the edge of a cliff. I did not jump off for I had heard something sick about what happens to you, dear, as you make your way down. So I said, dear dear dear dear dear dear dear dear and I screamed and I was making something. It was raining and I was very young. I knew you were there. I wasn't going to wait for you again. You you you you. Of special significance is the temperature of the bottom-left, where the near infrared binary star is the artefact. I was going to give you the features of the solid Earth and say everything. I was going to start with Monday and just see how we got along.

The trick is to not ... the trick is to have no ... the trick is to ... the trick is you ... the trick is you ... the trick is the ... the trick is ... the trick is ... the trick is ... the trick is thermometers but in the shape and style of a gun.

VIII

You were kind to me and I was ready for you after a long time of waiting. I had been breathing. I had been breathing for all those years. I had been engaged in a highly complex process since the day I was born. I wasn't even interested in 1963. Who was even there? I am not even interested in her hanging body which didn't protest when I pushed open the door. Of course I went in! I mean I wasn't even bothered about it. I could have taken or left 1963. It was of no concern to me. What of other years? I could take or leave other years, I was no historian, I was no medical expert, I was not a scientist or a lark. I was not a Godwit flying from the Arctic for eleven days straight. I was not a sudden jump in the animation. I was not a hoola hoop. I was not a link or a current event or a call to donate or a click. I was not a desk or a lamp. I was not wedges. I was a woman taking down another woman off a line. Eventually. It took me thirty years. By then I was strong enough for her. I had all her strength and I used it against her. By that time, she looked better suited to a life in a sea that might obscure her face, so blue, the rest of her perfect, the scarf was incredibly dark with blood. This I did not expect. There are surprises everywhere. It was obviously spring, there was wattle in the air the fan was going (?) a car was starting up some bird called. All these things were clear as I rifled through the kitchen drawers for a pair of scissors to cut the scarf. And I did cut it. She came down in a hump. And her face did not clear but I positioned myself on the floor. I got myself into this particular position.

IX

We were on the floor and the most important thing was the weight of her. She was still warm this was her blood which was also my blood you test us we're the same family. We are still. Let me finally tell you. You see I on the floor with my arms on the floor I positioned her body, oh it was deliciously heavy my chest under her arms behind her back. Her head was heavy it flopped her arms were heavy they flopped like all those years ago like history like chemical science like 1963 like the constellation heavy heavy heavy weight weight weight warm warm warm. I positioned myself behind her holding her I had these strong arms I positioned myself on the floor I positioned my body underneath her body I held her from behind under her arms her back was broad and warm where was our mother I would have to send a text to her a telegram a bird. I would have to send a message inside of the atmosphere to every true thing which was not a figment of these two bodies on the floor. I rocked her on the floor. Maybe I hummed a little but I didn't make any real noise. I definitely put my face to her neck her bloodied neck dried a little, caked. I held what I could hold of her I wrapped around her I rocked and rocked I slept I said maybe you'll like it.

X

I was horrified to learn that a large group of stars bound by gravitational pull is called a star *cluster* and I wanted to move on very quickly from my personal life. What was so personal about it? So far I had said everything. I hadn't done anything. I just breathed the air. I had a woman in my arms but she was dead. There wasn't an opportunity to have a feeling about it. Such death. Death does not tolerate feelings. Death is not a funeral. Death is not a party or a book launch. Death is continuation. Death is a line. Death is an incredible. Death is a sophistication. Death is an inexact science. Death is not a label. Death is not a Van Gogh. Death is not a solution. Death is not a powerhouse. Death is not an episode. Death is not a number. Death is not a degree. However we wept was of no significance and I am afraid with no good reason three three three three.

XI

Disambiguation is the removal of uncertainty or confusion. Countable and uncountable, it is clarification, enlightenment, illumination. A single star and a temperature measure. What a roost! Here is a spot of blood. It is too convenient. She is not even crying now. She is kind of listless but she is cool to the touch. You go about your lives until one day in 1963. What happened then? It was only a year but it was the beginning.

XII

You have to think about it differently. For example, a component of amino acids and urea. You have to think about it the same — that everything is made up of something. Something smaller. Like those dolls. Where is Russia! I have to make another cup of coffee to deal with this present day situation which I did not even ask for. Who *ordered* this? I cannot absolve geography into the merry system also seen with an interstellar probe everything is roughly forty minutes away in this city. It is a city with trees. It is a propulsion, a navigation. It is a camp site. It is a fire. It is a fugue.

But, like, is it a blue cube or is it a hexagon filled with three lines? These are the spaces. And what is the number 7? Nobody is coming for you. How would you break that down? You could break it down to ones but how are ones made up? Are ones a concept? I need to know such things to understand the material of waiting for you and loving you and breaking you and losing you. I broke you myself I guess I mean there wasn't anyone else here to do it.

But I did everything! I took every single breath! A breath happens singly! This is not interesting! We are not the same! You can be mindful or rash but it happens all the same! You can state the obvious! Who needs a pat? Who is itchy? Who is sad? You don't stop it happening unless you hold on to it. Shop now. Distraction. You hold it, all the sevens. You hold it, all the lines. The blue lines that make the flat, fragmented hexagon or that make the cube if you soften your gaze and you were good at Magic Eyes and you were good at black holes and I remember you but you're not an apple or a character. In this. I remember your blue sweater and your blue scarf and how you hanged yourself on the back of the front door in 1963 and we all stood around the whole lot of us and planted a tree when you did it again and did it for the last time because this was the arrangement thank you *so* much. You you you you. Hold it off. It could have been any number of you! Don't talk about it but watch the tree.

XIII

With regards to the seven the tree has been waiting a long time. It is a headache. No one is exactly prepared for it. Subscribe now. The electron configuration means something. How does a tree take it in? How much is in an actual tree? Is it a rolling commentary? Regulate your emotions. Don't be scared now. Try not to rape anybody. Rape is just a feeling. Subscribe now to a long long history of rape rape rape rape. Of silence. Of sticky sex. Of horror. Of lust. Of decree. Of passion. Of confusion. Of bright. Of books. Of blood. Of agony. Of worship. Of hollow. Of carving. Of brilliant. Of whole. Of hole. O O O O. I looked up and it was dark.

XIV

Nevertheless the tree. A special moment. 1963. Or: anywhere. A blue sweater. A black hole. All the girls were in blue sweaters but yours was different. We went to a good school! You bitch! You are not a princess! You are not a pink watch! You are not a Matisse! You are not Paris or Rome! You are not Egypt! You are not water! And a billion kilometres distance from the Sun is a reasonable distance and how far you are and I said I would wait I said I would go where you go I magic bastard I mistress I containment I restraint I liar you mysterious thief! I said I said I said I said I said I said I would be waiting for you! And the waiting happens backward as well as forward! At the same time!

About four-fifths of Earth's atmosphere is nitrogen. 1772. Fire air is supported by combustion and the other is foul air. When fire air is used up foul air returns. Potassium nitrate is KNO and a 3. You can easily make it

148

KNOw if you turn it all around and sharpen the edges and the sides and then you can understand it. Among the elements, nitrogen ranks sixth in cosmic abundance. It's not even a ribbon. You just missed out on that. Soon soon soon soon ... I've been waiting for you and you have not come. Well I'll come to you. I'll come immediately. This will be the movement and the nature. The motion will make the response the answer to the question of potential possibility regarding chaos. I've been *waiting* for you. That's the simple truth of it. And it is so simple. I've been waiting for you and breathing the air. My stomach hurts. I know this pain. We are all woman here.

XV

My stomach hurts. It goes around the back. You do not always have to pay for it. Words are a key and a signal and a box. My heart is throbbing. That's a real thing. Who was in the birthing suite? Who was in the bathing suit? I believe it was temporarily red. Who was in the waiting room? Where was she? Your father was somewhere in America. Hence the Americanisation of the sentence structure. Vocabulary. This is not cultural but it is interstellar. This is not racist but it is a minority of affluence and privilege related to a special hail and access to a stolen PC. Access to language? Put it in the veins, honey. Send it in a GIF. Don't be too true. I struggle to identify the use of it. Words are a concrete wall for putting the head into. Put it in *first*. Crush the skull and fill the egg with the clots of your personal history. For example, free nitrogen is found in many meteorites and this has been declared worldwide. Who is She, this world? What is *She* doing here? She liked the dinosaurs and the walking fish and then there was us. She had a thing for whales but she coloured them orange. Orange! We came along. She invented us. We could do anything. We did it together. It was up to her and me and you. Well somewhat him. It was organised and we followed procedure. It was equal parts scientific and natural. We filled our goody bags with free nitrogen from the gases in volcanos, mines and some mineral springs also. How does one make sense of this? Flicker flicker. We discovered her location. We put a word on her. We stuck a name on her like a button or a pin. Nobody can sew a button anymore. And in some stars are nebulae.

We can't go on like this!

I promised you I was breathing the air and I *meant* it. I took it in and I *expelled* it. I took in nineteen per cent *other stuff*. Air isn't just a gas. It holds a lot of other particles. The flame dances and the black daffodil ascends. It looks wispy but purposeful. It is reaching to nine o'clock. The tea is cold. That's the time for leaving. The air can carry sad things too. I am making my way to you. I am coming right now. I promised you I would come. You went on ahead. Someone sent balloons to the hospital. Someone sent an obese, completely unidentifiable soft toy. Under autopsy it was determined to be a fish. It had died from cotton and twine and also of being out of the water but it wasn't a metaphor. We laughed. They removed the tubes. For a time we were breathing the same air, you and me. We ate jelly and we breathed.

XVI

You say it's on the air but it's not on the air it's inside of it. But it is never inside it is always moving away from the dancing flame. I was frightened because people need to breathe. And so do other animals. And also plants. Carbon dioxide in the air can have a sad or happy face and red wings. Like labia. Why does everything smell of a ghost and sex? I guess that was not the making of you and now it wants to come after me. Sex. I mean they were definitely blood red. The doctor said flick a band or hold ice or smash plates from the second-hand store but be careful not to cut yourself. On the shards. That would defeat the purpose.

XVII

I am an old woman. Photosynthesis is fine. I taught our brother this. Everybody is dead. There isn't any truth in this. There are no lies. There was a yellow lounge. We lost him. I said green green green green. We lost lost lost him. And he understood everything. Like (weirdly) what we give is what's so sick and the power plants give it too but not the actual plants. She was learning about the location and the setting and about general motion. How much water can she hold before she rains? And all of that time I was putting out little toys I pulled desperately from anywhere like a magician when the magic was so obviously elsewhere.

This was a moment in our ordinary life.

XVIII

I was taking her in in a greedy manner, this is completely true. I was not cooperating. She was swarming from the insides, the apple is not a character, the telephone is not a portal, the digit is not a gas, the blanket is not a catastrophe or a statement of fact but the air changes as you go up up up up and that is completely true. That's called a special sickness to do with air and to do with going up. People climb mountains. That's their fun game. They do not have words for what is wrong at first. It seems a new thing.

XIX

Air seems light but there is a lot of it pushing down on the Earth's surface. I was taking in what I could in order to sort of lighten the load and also as something to do while I waited for her. I was not located in a place or a plot or a setting. You couldn't read between the lines. You couldn't listen to the same song over and over. There wasn't an obvious path forward. You looked at your hands but your hands weren't anything. I wasn't beyond the story but I wasn't in the middle of it and I couldn't narrate it. This is my best effort. By the time you get this I will be gone.

XX

All of the normal time you are experiencing high air pressure. The higher you climb the lower it goes. An interstellar probe would make this visible, the pushing. You push push push push but this is such an early stage in things and then you just have to hold on.

XXI

The air is a warm jacket is a blue sweater. Otherwise we would be so cold! They also protect us from the meteoroids. A meteoroid comes along made of fluff and junk. But like a billion cars and elephants contained in concrete coming for us. They rub rub rub, this giant soft ball. It is slippery wet for the concrete has not yet set. The air rubs the meteoroid. The meteoroid rubs the air. Rub rub rub rub rub. Her pretty eyes are closed. Rub rub rub rub – let me do this. Here. I'll be the atmosphere. You be the meteoroid. Rub rub rub rub, you burn, you explode. The Earth doesn't feel a thing.

XXII

Green smiles with umbrellas like fruits in hot air balloons are bioaerosols which live in the air. Wave to the soot the dust the pollen and the good things. Some things terminate on a branch of the cherry blossom tree. They never have sex don't know how to send a proper text message do not develop a psychiatric disorder even when the wind carries them miles from their original home. They have never heard of scarves do not own doors have never been slaves wave bye bye to the plantations as they pass over the other countries woven baskets on their backs filthy hands up and down. Mines explosions temperatures rashes limbs askew and askance blind deaf and dumb not moving or walking or eating you you you you. That's life on the planet until it goes in startling fashion and the next thing comes along and that's the dinosaurs who did not complain.

Next: Ten Interesting Things About Water.

XXIII

The Sextenary, or ADS9731, is a star system that consists of six stars. It is a planetary arrangement like the Lunar New Year. Four of the stars are visually separate in the sky. No planets have yet been detected in the system. My feet are cold. My fingers are cold. I am here on the brink. I am waiting for you.

The pressure is very high. The air is full of bugs and fluff. I thought I saw a big black creature on the ceiling this morning but it was only the button pressing the light fitting to the ceiling and I just had never seen it in that specific light before. Because less and less is actually going into my lungs and I look for her I look and she is not anywhere. She is gone.

XXIV

Because the uterus is much closer to the Earth we can draw better pictures, pull it apart, womb is the everyday context, the uterus has a neck, I nuzzle your uterus neck, I put my face into it, I trace your uterine cavity with the tip of my little finger I suck your placenta I swallow I push my nose like a hungry pup into the smooth muscle of your myometrium I investigate your junctional zone with my tongue. Watch your fingers, child. Smell the *dis*-ease. Lift your smooth stone grey fingers to your small, creature nose. Brittle the silk hairs. We are all woman here.

XXV

And I was gloating.

And it was perhaps because I gloated. Because I purchased a car. Because I started a degree or finished one. Because my shoelace was undone. Because I did not go to school. Because I worked in a shop. Because I grubbed. Because I did not buy a dog. Because I had money. Because I did not have money. Because I gave the dog away. Because I fed her broccoli pumpkin spinach croissants. Because I picked my head and ate it. Because I brushed my hair. Because my vagina was ugly. Because I was ashamed. Because I told her all my secrets because I didn't tell her them because I protected her. Because my skin was wrong and my body and I gave that to her. Because I did not protect her. Because she made a decision one day. Because she did not consult the stars she did not drop out she did not secure it. My toes are cold the tips of my fingers are cold everything is going this way everything is going in the one direction that makes us no different that makes us extremely the same, not sinister, politics has nothing to do with it, this is just a system this is just a country this is just a moment this is just a body under the stars.

Well, two.

Consider the stars.

XXVI

I rocked her and rocked. We were two women on the floor. The door was not yet open. Soon they would arrive. Nothing was over yet. Nothing was started. I had not put the dinner on. Nothing was finished at all. I did not protect her. I loved her all my life.

XXVII

It is not late. It is not over yet. I told her simply, I will wait for you on the other side of this impossible mess. I will wait for you I will hold you I will wait for you, terribly.

XXVIII

And so I held her like this and that's her story and she lives inside of mine and there is no hope in it and there is no fury and there is no woman and there is no body and there is no girl and there is no one else there is no story there is no forgiveness there is no calm there is no cruelty there is no reason there is no purpose there is no nearness there is no distance she is nowhere to be seen there is only this air and this body and these trees there is only this room there is only this love and it is not a living thing but it is like the wind it does not live this love it does not live but it breathes. Steady as the stars, my friend. My woman my mother my daughter my son. Steady as the stars except for the ones that flicker that sparkle that dance that fall that roar roar roar roar roar towards us.

Acknowledgements are due to my agent Jane Novak; Ed Wright and the team at Puncher and Wattmann; the Gadigal people of the Eora Nation, where these stories were written; and the following journals in which certain of these stories have appeared: *Antipodes, the Long Paddock & Overland.*

www.ingramcontent.com/pod-product-compliance
Lightning Source LLC
Chambersburg PA
CBHW031311280626
47169CB00018B/1235